KALIFAX

KALIFAX

DUNCAN THORNTON

COTEAU BOOKS

Edited by Geoffrey Ursell.
Cover image and interior illustrations by Yves Noblet.
Cover and book design by Duncan Campbell.

Printed and bound in Canada.

Canadian Cataloguing in Publication Data

Thornton, Duncan, 1962—
Kalifax
ISBN 1—55050—152—6

I. Title.

PS8589.H556K34 1999   jC813'.54   C99—920142—5
PZ7.T3936Ka 1999

10   9   8   7   6   5   4

COTEAU BOOKS

401-2206 Dewdney Ave
Regina, Saskatchewan
Canada   S4R 1H3

AVAILABLE IN CANADA AND THE US FROM:
Fitzhenry & Whiteside
195 Allstate Parkway
Markham, Ontario
Canada   L3R 4T8

The publisher gratefully acknowledges the financial assistance of the Saskatchewan Arts Board, the Canada Council for the Arts, the Government of Canada through the Book Publishing Industry Development Program (BPIDP), and the City of Regina Arts Commission, for its publishing program.

For Brenda Anne,
who heard it first.

Table of Contents

THE VOYAGE NORTH

THE TRIAL OF THE ICE

THE LONG WAY HOME

List of Illustrations

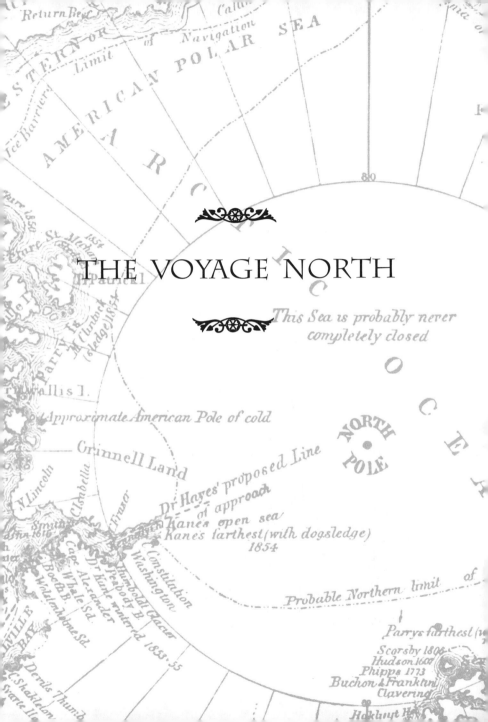

THE VOYAGE NORTH

She tossed up a new tinderbox, right into Tom's hands

CHAPTER ONE:
TOM'S STORY

"WE'LL SAIL NORTH, TO THE EAVES OF THE World," the Captain said. "It's dark and cold under the rafters of the sky, and great and strange beasts live squeaking in those high corners, out of the reach of men and women, but we'll sail into the eaves and shoulder through the icy narrows of the sea and then drop down the other side of the West into spice winds and warm waters and lazy islands that bloom like summer flowers.

"Who'll come with me?"

"Skating on the ice till you freeze, that's what it would be," one grizzled sailor said. "And poor vittles in the meantime."

The others thought for a moment. "Strange beasts?" one of the other sailors said.

"Squeaking?" one of the sailors said.

"Ice trolls and snow-goblins!" a third one shouted.

"Winds so cold they burns your skin!"

"Winds that screams with ghost voices!" moaned two sailors in the corner.

"Fire that dances in the black night sky!" cried Tom.

That made them keep quiet.

"Strange beasts, ice trolls, snow-goblins, winds so cold they burns your skin and screams with ghost voices of the other people whose skins they's burnt, and squeaking, I've heard tell of many a time," said the oldest sailor, while he tied his neckcloth in a bowline, just to keep in practice. "But I've never heard of fire that dances in the black night sky. You wouldn't just be telling a tale, young Tom?"

"No, sir," young Tom said. "My Dad told me."

THEY ALL LISTENED while Tom told his story:

"When the elves lived here a long time ago, two elves had a magic torch called Kalifax. Kalifax could burn so bright that roosters crowed; it could burn so hot that rocks would wilt.

"The two elves went North to climb to the Roof of the World, and the ice was cold, but they had Kalifax to keep them warm. They kept going North until they heard strange beasts squeaking, but they had Kalifax to scare them away.

"They went North until they saw the lights of the goblins gathering, but they had Kalifax to warn them back. They went North until they felt the winds so cold they burns you while they scream with ghost voices –"

"Ahh! The cold winds with the ghost voices!" cried the two sailors in the corner.

"But they had Kalifax, so they were fine," said Tom.

"They went North until they were by the very Peak of

2

the North, where there was a great mountain of ice that stretched into the sky, where it touched to the Roof of the World."

"At the Peak of the North, they heard ice trolls muttering close, but they had Kalifax to drive them off. By then they were very cold, but they had Kalifax to keep them warm, and they started to climb the mountain of ice. But when they were halfway up the mountain, Turiel said, 'I might perish from the cold, even with Kalifax.'

"And when they were three-quarters of the way up the mountain, Firiel said, 'I might perish from the cold, even with Kalifax.'

"And at the very peak of the mountain, with the Roof of the World above their heads, they lay down beside one another and began to fall asleep from the cold, even with Kalifax.

"Then Kalifax burned brighter than it had ever burned before, until the Queen of the Hall of the Stars saw Kalifax burning, and looked down and saw Turiel and Firiel lying together asleep from the cold, and sent her servants to bring them up to her Hall, where they still are.

"And she put Kalifax above the door to her Hall, and in the Eaves of the World you can see its flames dancing in the black night sky. My Dad says," said Tom.

"WELL, I'LL COME WITH YOU," the oldest sailor said to the Captain, as he stood up and thumped the floor with his peg leg. "We don't have to go all as high North as the elves, after all, and there'll be sights to see and fire that dances in the black night sky, and when we drop down the other side of the West, there'll be spice winds and warm waters, and lazy islands that bloom like summer flowers."

"You'll be my First Mate," said the Captain.

All the other sailors leapt up and said they'd come too, even if they weren't elves.

"And confusticate the ice trolls!" cried one sailor.

"And woe betide the snow-goblins!" cried another.

"And malefy the cold winds that screams with ghost voices!"

The two sailors in the corner shivered at that part, but they came too.

Only the grizzled old sea hand, who, as a consequence of also having a wooden leg, was a friend of the First Mate, had kept quiet. "And what'll you eat?" he demanded now. "Cold porridge and icicle biscuits all the way?"

"What would you make instead?" the First Mate asked.

"Well – well, a nice warm *burgoo,* for starters, considering the nature of the Exploration. And steaming *calabash,* and piping hot *Wgee,* and –"

"You'll be our Cook," the Captain said.

"Well, all right," the Cook said, "but after we all freeze stiff, you're on your own."

The Captain nodded with satisfaction. "Twenty

4

stout sailors, then," he said. "A whole crew."

"And me!" said Tom.

"Twenty-one for good luck," the Captain said with a smile. "You'll be our Kalifax."

TOM LIVED IN A HARBOUR VILLAGE where feats of mighty sailing were much admired, but his friend Jenny was crabbed that his Dad had said he could go and did not congratulate him.

"I am *not* jealous that you are after leaving on a maritime Exploration of great daring while I must remain here and every day merely gather in my nets," she explained while they sat in her fishing dory, bobbing in the waves. (And Jenny was always a great one for explaining, though she had an odd way of speaking, because she lived by herself and read so much, and worked with all manner of crusty old fishers and sailors.)

"For not uncommonly," Jenny continued, "a caught flounder will grant three wishes to a fisher who lets it go, and though none of the flounder I catch have yet spoken, when one does I will ask for: First, my own ship – which I shall name *Nonesuch,* for it shall be paramount, without peer, and simply tip-top in all respects – and a crew for it; and second, a chart to find the lost city that sank beneath the waves; and thirdly, I will ask for my prize expanding telescope back, which fell beneath the sea yesterday while I looked for schools of flounder."

The Voyage North

"You lost your prize telescope!" Tom exclaimed. "I'm sorry."

"And now I'm after losing my friend to an Exploration, although once I find the lost city that sank beneath the waves and gain fame and riches, our paths may cross on the vast ocean. You will know me because I shall be wearing a tricorn hat and standing on the prow of the *Nonesuch,* except in rough waters, when I shall take the wheel myself."

Tom looked at Jenny, who was sitting in the bow of the little boat, pointing her chin proudly to the West.

"I might not see you until next summer," Tom said.

"You might not see me until the summer after that," Jenny said, still out of sorts, "since you have not only to circumnavigate the globe, itself reputed to be an under-taking of substantial length, but first to find your way through the icy seas of the cold dark North, that no one yet has done."

Tom was quiet for a moment, listening to the wheel-ing gulls call under the dull grey sky. "How long do you think it will be before we find our way home?" he asked.

"I think you may find your doom in the icy North, whether by cold or goblinry, or bands of trolls or, perhaps, the cold again," Jenny told him, "and never find your way back to be my friend at all, unless I sail to your rescue in the *Nonesuch,* which moment would be a fine one, full of much glory and satisfaction."

And Tom thought it would be a fine moment too, except that the *Nonesuch* was only in Jenny's imagination, whereas even now the Captain's ship was being provisioned for the icy North, because he had told the story of Kalifax.

THE CAPTAIN'S SHIP HAD AN ELF NAME; it was called *Volantix*. And the next day, Tom asked permission to board the *Volantix* and speak with him.

The Captain's cabin was papered over with charts of the Seven Seas and Tom stared at them for a moment. They were coloured in blues and greens and browns, except the Northern one, the one for their Exploration.

"Is the Northern chart white because it shows ice and snow, or because it is all unknown?" Tom asked.

"Because it shows ice and snow, and because it is all unknown," the Captain said. "Young Tom, you seem troubled."

"Yes, sir," Tom said. "For now I don't know if I want to come on the Exploration anymore."

And Tom told the Captain all that Jenny had said, not mentioning the dire words of the Cook, which troubled him as well.

Then the Captain was silent. "All those dangers are true," he said at last, "and many others not mentioned or foreseen. Your far-seeing friend is right to warn you."

"Really?" Tom said.

"Yes, really," the Captain said. He rolled up a map and put it away in a pigeonhole. "Young Tom," he said, "when you told the story of Kalifax, this Exploration began; now

N

7

leave its finish to the rest of us."

Tom nodded slowly. "Will you be back by next summer?" he asked.

"With luck," the Captain said. Then suddenly he grinned.

"With luck," he said again. "And with fair winds, and a feat of mighty sailing such as the world has never known, by next summer we'll have shouldered through the icy narrows of the sea and then dropped down the other side of the West into spice winds and warm waters and lazy islands that bloom like summer flowers, and so come home, as no one yet has done. And because of your words, the *Volantix* will be the glory of the Northern world."

For a moment Tom looked at the white chart again, considering all the Captain had said. "I'm sorry," he said at last, "I do want to come, if you will have me back."

"You burn bright in danger," the Captain said. "You are like Kalifax. Tell your father all, and if he says yes a second time, you may come, and shall be our hope."

THE HULL OF THE *Volantix* was painted in checks of red and blue, and above that a line of green that rose and fell like the waves of the sea. High above rose the great mainmast, its sails all neatly furled, and the mizzen-mast behind it.

"Have we got everything?" the Captain asked from the prow, where he'd been polishing the figurehead, which was a carving of the Queen of the Hall of the Stars.

"There's no nanny goat for milk, cheese, and curds," the Cook said. Then he muttered, "Not that the poor beast will survive, what with the cold and all." But the others affected not to hear him.

"We'll want more salt meat," one of the other sailors said.

"And pots of port wine," one of the sailors said.

"Lots of lanterns for the cold dark nights!" a third one shouted from the yardarm.

"And more swords just in case!" cried the two sailors on the poop deck.

"Find a nanny goat for milk, cheese, and curds; and load more salt meat, pots of port wine, lots of lanterns for the cold dark nights, and more swords just in case!" the Captain ordered.

"And lemon pies," added the First Mate. The parrot he carried on his shoulder squawked in excitement at that.

"Lemon pies!" repeated the parrot (it was an especially ornamental green and red kind). "Lemon pies! Ding-dong! Awk!"

"And thick wool mittens and long, knit scarves!" said Tom's Dad, who'd come to watch the provisioning.

"That's a wise suggestion, Sir," the Captain said. "Bring scarves and mittens too."

ALL THE WHILE THE CREW OF THE *Volantix* was preparing for the voyage, the other seafarers and fishers, and all their relations, which is to say the whole town, grew more excited, and presented them with goodbye dinners and farewell parties and good luck songs by the score. So after a week, the *Volantix* and all her sailors too were full almost to bursting, and Tom himself could hardly sleep from anticipation.

And as for Tom's dog, he knew something was up, but couldn't decide whether to bark all the time, for excitement, or lie with his paws over his head, for he was sure to be left behind. So he settled on doing both, one after the other, as a compromise.

At last came a morning when the *Volantix* lay ready. The ship rocked gently in its moorings, smelling of tar and new rigging, and fresh paint. "Titivations complete," reported the First Mate, who had a weakness for fine language, and only meant they were done making the ship pretty.

Overhead, the clouds sailed high under a fair spring wind. The Captain waved his cocked hat in the air. "Last goodbyes!" he called. "And all aboard!" And all the crew felt their hearts beat faster.

Tom's friend Jenny said goodbye from her little fishing dory as it bobbed in the water beside the *Volantix*. "Though I'm so sad and dischuffed I can hardly speak," she called across the water, "for it is only a week since I lost my prize expanding telescope in the sea, and now I'm losing my friend to a long Exploration.

"I am not jealous," Jenny said again, still holding forth

from her dory, "but I am curt with sorrow, and not a little worried that you will be without me to counsel and inspirit you. So take care, and be stout and resourceful." Then she tossed up a new tinderbox, right into Tom's hands. "And mind this present," she said, "which is in case you find yourself shrammed and chill in some wintry harbour with no other means to make fire."

Tom looked down at the tinderbox and waited until he thought he understood all the things Jenny had said. Then he called back, "Thank you!" And after a moment or two, he added, "Fine weather and full nets." (Which was thought the proper way to say goodbye to fishers.)

Jenny had considered at length the best thing to say to someone leaving on a risky Exploration. "Accurate charts and helpful strangers," she replied.

N

II

THEN TOM TOLD HIS DOG NOT TO WORRY, but to behave, and do as Jenny told him until he came back, and said goodbye to him too.

Last of all Tom and his Dad said goodbye, and then the sailors had work to do.

And as they hauled on the capstan to raise the anchor, the crew sang to keep their time:

> With a heave, ho! and it's North we go,
> To the Eaves of the World and the icy Xow!
> With a heave to! and we'll make it through,

The Voyage North

Till we Wnd the home of the cockatoo!
With a heave, haul! and it's one for all,
And cry woe betide should the goblins call!

As the work grew harder the words of their song slowed down:

Heave, lads, haul, Tom,
Till the ropes are straining!
Haul, lads, heave, Tom,
For the Captain's waiting!

And when the capstan began to turn freely once more their words came quicker again:

With a heave, ho! and it's North we go,
To the Eaves of the World and the icy Xow!
With a haul, heave! for its South we seek,
Where the warm winds blow and the trees are teak!
But now heave, ho! Wrst it's North we'll go,
Through the Eaves of the World and the icy Xow!

Then the anchor was raised and fished, sailors ran up the rigging and let go the sails, and soon the *Volantix* began to creak and rock, underway at last. As they cleared the harbour, Tom's Dad called, "Goodbye!" and then everyone on shore began cheering.

Even as the wind filled the sails, and long after they

had left the quay far behind, Jenny rowed alongside the ship until, slowly, slowly at first, the *Volantix* began to leave her behind. Jenny stopped rowing then and waved goodbye one last time, as the ship sailed faster, pulling Northwest under fair skies,

The *Volantix* sailed faster still, faster till the sea parted beneath its bow in long white curls. Faster until the sailors began to shout for joy, even the two sailors on the poop deck, until Tom lost sight of Jenny in the distance.

AT FIRST THEY OFTEN MET FISHING BOATS. Gulls looped over the boats, looking for scraps, and high above them bright white clouds drifted in the tall blue sky. Tom would wave from the crow's nest where he kept watch, and the people on the fishing boats would wave back with their fish.

As they kept on North the boats grew fewer and the spray grew colder, and for a week or more all Tom saw from his lookout were lonely little islands where only puffins lived. But on one island there were whalers too, and the *Volantix* made harbour – "The last harbour before we drop down the other side of the West," the Captain said.

For the Puffin Island whalers were the most Northerly sailors the Captain knew, and some of them had been towed almost to the Eaves of the World by harpooned whales. So while Tom played catch-herring with the children, and the sailors caroused in the manner of sailors on shore, the Captain and the First Mate made long and elaborate consultations with the whalers. But the advice they kept hearing from the old Northern hands was usually the same: *"Don't go,"* or *"Leave sooner."*

And when the Captain asked for recommendations if they *did* go now, rather than sooner, the old Northern hands would pull at their beards and mutter to one another in their own language, and finally come up with something like: "Give up as early as you can."

But some of them had practical advice too, and the Captain and the First Mate listened carefully, while they waited for the summer to grow stronger and clear the ice from their way. At last, when they had learned everything they could, they hoisted the blue peter, the blue flag with a white square in the middle, which tells sailors their ship is ready to leave.

The next morning the crew gathered by the *Volantix*, looking much the worse for wear, and less happy to hear that there were new crates to be hauled aboard, "Just in case," the Captain said.

"In case of what?" Tom asked.

The First Mate gave him a discouraging look. "In case we need them," he said, adjusting a new peg leg he'd had fitted by the whalers. "And now let's all get busy, for you've spent your money and stayed up late for days and days. It's time to be back on the sea and in the clean cold air."

The Voyage North

So the *Volantix* steered Northwest again, and Tom resumed his station in the crow's nest, though there was little to see.

But one day he spied a sad and weather-beaten boat steered by a romantic young man dressed in black trousers and a baggy white shirt. Tom waved to him too. "We're sailing North to the Eaves of the World!" Tom shouted.

"I'm sailing to get away!" the young man shouted back.

"Get away from what?" Tom called.

"From the lonely World!" the romantic young man shouted, before going below decks in a funk.

The *Volantix* kept on, and soon the sailors breathed out clouds of frost and the spray of the waves was sharp with ice. "So far, so good," the Captain said, while the First Mate finished putting a ship in bottle, "but keep an eye for any trouble, young Tom."

But there was a long stretch yet of fair sailing, and Tom saw no trouble from high in his lookout, only once in a while an Irish saint bobbing through the icy water in a little leather boat. Tom would wave and shout, "We're sailing to the Eaves of the World!"

"Bless you!" they'd shout back. "You'll need it."

15

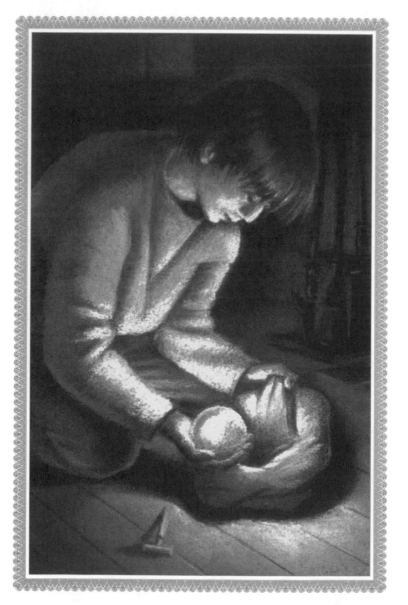

"I found the last of my presents from Grandfather Frost"

CHAPTER TWO:
THE CAPTAIN'S STORY

So the *Volantix* sailed North and West until the summer turned. Usually the afternoons were still warm enough, but the evening chill came quickly. And every day the sun grew smaller, just as the seas grew colder.

One day, when the ropes and the sails had grown rimy with ice, and all the sailors were wearing the scarves and mittens Tom's Dad had told them to bring, Tom saw the Captain and the First Mate by the binnacle that housed the ship's compass, bending their heads together over their charts. The First Mate was knitting a warmer sweater while they talked, and the Captain's beard was furred with frost.

Then the First Mate whistled and all the sailors gathered together to listen right away sharp. "Tom and all you sailors," the Captain said while the First Mate carried on with his knitting, "we've come as North as we know where to be, and now our maps have stopped and our exploring has begun. Watch for trouble and keep your swords close."

The Cook had a gloomy disposition, after so many years of making fine dishes only to see them spoiled by storms or other maritime hazards. So as he served up dinner that night, he announced, "We're half lost, already."

The First Mate, long used to his friend's gloomy ponderations, rolled his eyes, but the two sailors from the poop deck wailed, "Lost! We're lost?"

"Half lost," the Cook said, as though he enjoyed repeating it. "We know how to go back, just not forwards, which is, nonetheless, what we're doing."

Tom could see the two sailors trying work out what that amounted to on their fingers. Just as they had it figured and were opening their mouths to begin moaning again, the Cook quieted them. "Wailing about it won't help you," he said. "Now eat your *lobscouse.*" And he put a steaming bowl of it in front of Tom.

Most of the Cook's dishes weren't nearly as bad as they sounded, but were either a strange sort of porridge or a rough sort of stew. *Lobscouse* was the stew kind.

FROM THEN ON Tom didn't see any other ships, and they lit more lanterns as the nights grew longer. It still got colder every day, and when the waves broke over the ship the spray turned to ice in the air and rattled down across the deck. But they were all alone in the sea until one night when Tom pointed and cried out: "Look!"

All the sailors rushed to the side of the ship to hold up their lanterns and peer ahead. By the glinting yellow light they could just see that the *Volantix* was slipping towards a great mountain of ice pushing up from beneath the silvery waves.

"Is that *the* Mountain?" young Tom asked, his eyes wide.

The First Mate had been holding up his parrot so it could see too, and now he put it back on his shoulder and started unrolling his charts.

"Is that the Mountain?" the parrot repeated, looking down at the charts. "Is it? Is it? Is that the Mountain? Is –"

"No," the Captain told Tom. *"We've* never seen its kind before, but look – up high, under the stars, you can see its peak easily enough. It seems great to us, but this is only an iceberg, a minnow among such things, not a whale."

Tom and the parrot and all the sailors nodded, and the Captain ordered that the sails be shortened and the First Mate take the helm. "Take us under the lee of the ice," the Captain said. "Not too close, for near these mountains of ice, frozen reefs lie beneath the waves, but not too far to see: for our maps are all come to an end and now we may find new wonders to draw on the margins."

Tom stood beside the Captain at the guardrail, and together they watched the iceberg slide away to starboard. "You have good eyes, young Tom," the Captain said, "and kept the *Volantix* from foundering on the ice. Shall I tell you how I knew this wasn't the mountain at the Peak of the North?"

Tom nodded, and the Captain pulled a ball of glass from beneath his cloak.

N

19

"LOOK CLOSE," THE CAPTAIN SAID, and then he told his story:

"When I was a boy, Grandfather Frost left many things in my stockings. Ice skates and pocket knives and thimbles and toy swords and books and toques with long tails, and whistles and tops, and butterscotch candy. And my mother and father, they left many things in my stockings too, sometimes in his name, remembering the many things Grandfather Frost had left them when they were small, and one of them was a little wooden ship, the *Swallow* I called her, that was my first command, but I lost her in the mighty creek that swept behind our home.

"I remember all the presents I found in my stockings, though most of them are gone now. For when you are small you learn to lose little things just as you learn to read short books, because when you are grown there will be long books to read, and harder things you will have to lose."

The Captain stopped then and looked at the Great Way rising high in the sea of stars above them, and the *Volantix*, sailing faster now, crested a wave in the stirring sea below them and the cold salt spray stung their faces.

"But at the end of my journeys, I hope to come to a place where all the things I've lost lie scattered, only waiting for me to gather them in my arms," he said, "and not least among them will be the *Swallow*."

The Captain turned away from the sea and bent down before Tom, still holding the ball of glass, and now Tom could see that it held stars too, glimmering from

20

the plummy depths of the globe.

"As I grew older," the Captain said, "my stockings held fewer whistles and candies, and more and more my mother and father would give me practical things a young man would need. And one year I thought I'd find no more toys and no more gifts from Grandfather Frost at all, and I pulled out from my stocking pens, and a razor, and brushes for polishing my boots; and then right at the toe I found this glass, the last of my presents from Grandfather Frost.

"Take it in your hand."

Tom took the glass and held it carefully in his hand. He looked closer and saw that beneath the miniature stars was a stretch of frozen land shining faintly in their tiny light.

"Now hold it to the North," the Captain said, and as Tom moved the ball of glass he saw that the stars inside changed, and when he held it right up to the North a great mountain of ice appeared inside the glass, right at the crook of the tiny night sky and the miniature frozen land.

"Whenever you hold the star-glass due North, you see the Mountain reaching up into the cold night sky," the Captain said. "Since I was a boy this last gift from Grandfather Frost has been my compass, and I've kept it safe. No coast I've known is more familiar to me than the shape of the Great Mountain I've seen in the glass. That is how I knew the iceberg wasn't the mountain at the Peak of the North, and that is how I knew your story about the elves was true."

The Voyage North

"My friend Jenny gave me a tinderbox for the Exploration," Tom said.

"That's a fine present," said the Captain, "and just the thing for a voyage to the cold dark North. Keep it tucked away safe."

TOM AND THE CAPTAIN were about to leave the rail when suddenly a long strange squeaking noise came sounding off the iceberg and the chill, night-black sea. The sailors all stopped straightaway.

There was another long squeak, and then another, and the awful squeaks echoed among the valleys of the iceberg until it seemed there were dozens. Then the noise stopped.

"Strange beasts!" the sailors on the poop deck moaned in the silence. "Strange beasts squeaking!" Then all you could hear was the chattering of their teeth.

Suddenly a great horn with a spiral of gold flashed out of the black sea and struck against the long spar at the prow of the *Volantix*.

"Oh-ho!" cried the Captain, drawing his sword. "A whale who wants to fence with us!"

Tom looked at the whale's great ivory and gold horn, a good twenty feet long, and then at the sword in the Captain's hand. The sword looked awfully small.

The First Mate and his parrot looked at the whale's great ivory and gold horn, and then at the sword in the

Captain's hand. Neither of them said anything, though the red feathers on the parrot's head twitched a few times.

The two sailors on the poop deck just looked at the whale and shivered. And the Cook crossed his arms and thought morosely of the fine soufflé he had in the oven, which seemed sure to be disturbed at a crucial moment, while some of the other sailors just nodded encouragingly toward the *smasher,* the great cannon on the foredeck, and hoped the Captain would take the hint.

But the Captain only looked at the great ivory and gold horn, flashing down beneath the waves and up again as the whale's smooth white body leapt half out of the water, and then at the sword in his hand.

The Captain started to laugh. "That's a fight I'd lose!" he said, sheathing his sword. "Hard about to port! We'll leave the whale master of these seas!" The First Mate turned the wheel and all the sailors rushed to trim the sails, laughing with relief.

Just as the *Volantix* began to lean away from the white sheen of the iceberg, Tom cried: "Look, I see more coming!" The Captain followed Tom's pointing arm and saw a half-dozen more bright horns, arcing towards the mountain of ice through the black sea.

The Captain waved his tricorn hat to the whale as it turned towards the newcomers. "You have the better of us," he shouted, "but here are more worthy swords coming your way! Good luck to you!" He laughed again.

The Voyage North

N

23

"That's a fight I'd have lost," he said, and went into his cabin to bed.

Now as the *Volantix* sailed on the sun slid ever lower in the sky, and even at suppertime, when the sailors were eating a hot dish of the porridge the Cook called *burgoo,* and holding steaming mugs of coffee and rum in their mittens, the sun hung so low in the Southern sky they had to stand up to see it over the rails.

"Soon we'll have left the sun's country altogether," the Captain said. "It's time to bear West."

A day came when the sky was already roses and violets as Tom climbed back up to the crow's nest after supper. The long night was making its earliest start yet, and Tom looked South, to a little spur of icy land that gleamed gold in the setting sun, and saw a thin string of smoke rising.

He pulled out his expanding telescope (not nearly as fine as the one Jenny had lost beneath the waves) and looked close for a long time. At last he made out two or three figures moving about on the shore, all bundled up in thick fur hoods and jackets, and far behind them a domed house of snow, glowing in the dusk from the light inside.

"Elves!" he called to the Captain, "I think I see elves!"

The Captain left the wheel and climbed quickly up the shrouds to just below the crow's nest. He leaned out, holding the rigging with one hand and looking through his own spyglass with the other. On the chilly deck below all the sailors had gathered around to hear what the Captain made of it.

"No," the Captain said, "those aren't elves, they are the Snow People, who live the farthest North of all human-kind. Look! They're waving to us."

Tom looked and saw them waving harpoons high in the twilight air. He waved a signal flag back as hard as he could.

"Those are the last mortal men and women we shall see until we drop down the other side of the West into spice winds and warm waters," the Captain said, just as the sun slid beneath the frosty rim of the sea and the long Arctic night settled over them.

"And that is the last of the summer."

N

25

The Voyage North

CHAPTER THREE:
THE SEA BEYOND
THE LAND WHERE
NO PEOPLE LIVE

So at last they had come to the Sea Beyond the Land Where No People Live, which lies under the Eaves of the World. The *Volantix* sailed West every day, and through the twilight, and into the long night, through seas that were narrow with ice.

The most dangerous part of their Exploration had begun.

To Tom especially, it seemed that they were creeping ever more slowly through an endless field of luminous ice. The coast away to the South was blasted and barren, and in the frozen waters they sailed the wind and the sea had carved and hollowed the ice into pillars and knolls and caves; a whole sea country of strange, round, winter shapes that glowed softly in the evening gloom.

Tom dressed up warmer every day, and the sailors stuffed the crow's nest with straw to keep him snug, but his cheeks still burned in the cold wind. He saw many fine things: strange beasts that appeared from nests in the ice for just a moment before they dove into the water, and white crusts of frozen sea that crowded and bumped against the fenders of old junk they'd hung round the ship to protect her sides, and best of all were whales blowing plumes of steam that turned to clouds of frost twinkling in the twilight air.

But while the sailors worked on deck or tended the sails and rigging, Tom always kept an eye out for trouble, and he always hoped they might have sailed close enough that he could have just a glimpse of the Great Mountain at the Peak of the North.

Tom often thought of what Jenny would say when he finally returned and told her the story of all he'd seen. *"That was well-sailed,"* he imagined her saying about the Great Mountain, *"to Wnd one prominence which so contains both frozen immensity and navigational signiWcance."*

Then, Tom thought, he would smile modestly, as befit someone returning from such an Exploration.

MORE THAN ONCE, as they passed a cliff of ice, they heard a terrible moaning, and a great piece of it, bigger than the *Volantix*, split off and crashed into the sea. *"Growlers,"* the First Mate called the giant frozen chunks, from the noise they made, and they were a terrible hazard to sailing.

And more than once, two great islands of ice crashed together and rose from the water like stags that had locked horns, and the boom they made swept across the sea and shook the deck of the *Volantix* until the two sailors on the

N

27

poop deck held each other and quivered like porridge in the morning.

Below decks, the Cook would nod sadly at the nanny goat, as if the noise was just what he'd been expecting all along.

Now the First Mate kept calm at these times, for he was occupied by projects. But he'd look up from whittling out a new pipe or crocheting a shawl for his parrot, or practising which eye it was better to have a patch over, and say, "There's no cause for alarm; I've heard tell of louder noises," which always reassured the other sailors.

Just the same, Tom observed that the Captain and the First Mate often talked seriously with their heads bowed close together. And one day when Tom went to ask a question about toy ships, he heard some of what the Captain was saying.

"I don't like this sailing in the long evenings and shortening days," the Captain said. "We stayed too long in the Puffin Islands and misjudged our time, and now the seas are grown too narrow and the sky is too long dark." The First Mate had his sextant out and had been trying to triangulate the Evening Star and the left ear of one of the sailors on the poop deck, but now he put down the instrument.

"We're in a race with Winter then," the First Mate said. "And here we are racing in the very place that Winter is strongest of any place on Earth. But maybe we can make it to open sea before he grabs us in his ice to stay."

"Maybe," the Captain said, and stopped because

N

28

he saw that Tom was there.

Tom blushed, thinking of what Jenny would say when she heard he'd listened in, but the Captain only said, "That's all right, Tom; you were surprised to hear such serious business. But this is your business too, so listen close. We need to sail as fast as ever we can, for the ice is closing in and could maroon us for the winter, and maybe the next summer, and the winter after that too, so use your young eyes hard and look out for open water."

The Captain nodded at the First Mate and said, "Tell the others."

Then the First Mate's parrot whistled, and the sailors gathered round to listen right away sharp. While the Captain stood beside him on the foredeck and looked down at the icy sea parting beneath the *Volantix*'s iron cutwater, the First Mate pulled off a frozen mitten and struck it against the rail so hard that it clattered and sent chunks of frost flying into the air.

"Tom and all you sailors!" he cried. "Listen now. We're in a race with Winter where Winter is strongest! We're chasing open water and any path to the West, and the cold is chasing us, and seeks any way to freeze us forever in the sea. Jump to the lines when you hear Tom's call, for it's mortal stakes and Winter's gaining!"

Now the *Volantix* pressed on through freezing seas that were full of peril and wonder. She sailed with all the speed her crew could manage, on and on through the night if there was even a scrap of starlight to steer her by. West past gloomy cliffs of ice and forest islands where ancient trees had turned to stone before the elves were born, and West through dark tribes of seals that swam like fish and barked like dogs.

If the sails were still for any length of time they grew a skin of ice, and when the ship tacked round and the wind caught them again they would shed their skin with a shiver and tinkle and tumble on the crew below.

That was miserable for the sailors, who were buffeted besides by the cold sea air until they wrapped their scarves around and held their mittens over their aching ears, but things were colder still for young Tom in the crow's nest.

Tom wrapped more warm clothes round himself every day – though their days were growing very short now – until only his head peeked out from a frosty hill of blankets and furs.

Half hidden by straw, with his face red from the cold sea wind, a thick scarf wound over his nose, and a warm toque with a long tail pulled over his ears, you would hardly have known it was Tom keeping watch at all. But even though Tom was scared because it was so cold, and because the ice was closing in, and because their race with Winter was grown so tight, he was still glad he was on the Exploration.

And he kept a sharp lookout for open sea, but the narrow channels gave them little choice in their heading, and if the wind blew from the wrong quarter, their progress was slow indeed. "Open water to the West-Northwest!" Tom would cry.

"Bear West-Northwest for open water!" the Captain would call to the First Mate and the orders would echo around the ship: "Hard about!" "Bend the jib!" "West-Northwest for open water!"

But as hard as they pressed, every day the days were shorter, the seas were narrower, the open water was harder to find, and the *Volantix* crept slower through the icy gloom.

THEN ONE DAY a terrible storm blew up, dark and cold.

The *Volantix* took shelter under the cliffs of a huge iceberg, almost the size of the one where they had met the whale with the great twisted horn, and as the winds began to whip, the Captain ordered Tom to climb down from the crow's nest before it became too dangerous.

They dropped anchors fore and aft and hoped one would catch in the icy harbour beneath the cliffs. As the wind began to buffet them the First Mate tucked his parrot under his coat and the crew rushed to furl the sails and lash down anything that could move.

The Captain shouted orders as loud as he could, but the storm pulled the words away before anyone could hear, and he had to trust his crew knew their work. Tom tried to keep out of the way, and he held his mittens over his ears to keep the cold wind out till his hands went numb.

The Voyage North

One of the sailors busy battening down the scuttles and hatches looked up as a powerful gust came and Tom just heard him cry, *"Winds so cold they burns your skin!"* And then the wind caught Tom and took him dancing over the rocking deck. He tripped and spun towards the port rail, all without wanting to, and hardly seeing, for the air had become a streak of snow and ice and freezing spray.

Then Tom struck the side, and pitched half over the rail. For a moment he hung helplessly, staring into the roiling darkness below. Then the black waves reached up for him and Tom began to slip over the side. At the last moment before he fell into the tumult of the cold salt sea, Tom felt the Captain's hand catch his shoulder and pull him back on deck.

Tom tried to say something, but his lips were too cold to speak, and then the Captain moved him towards the last open hatch. "Get below, Tom!" the Captain shouted in his ear. "We'll all follow; it's our death to be outside!"

Tom stumbled down into the hold and huddled by the stove. One by one the rest of the sailors followed him. Stunned by the storm, they looked around the crowded galley at one another. The *Volantix* rocked harder and harder with each blast of wind, and the Cook's pots rang as they crashed overhead, but they were all safely inside, even the two sailors from the poop deck. "But where are the Captain and the First Mate, who found us all and got us safely below?" Tom asked.

For the Captain and the First Mate had stayed above

to make sure no one was forgotten. But now at last they appeared together at the top of the ladder, stiff with cold and all white with ice. And just as they bolted the last hatch behind them, the hardest blast of all hit the *Volantix*.

The blast came so hard the sailors tumbled together on the floor, and the Captain and the First Mate, and the First Mate's parrot, flew down the stairs and landed among them. The blast came so hard it blew out three portholes with a lash of water that struck the sailors so hard they yelled with pain. Worst of all, the blast came so hard it sucked the air from the lanterns and knocked the fire from the stove, so the whole crew of the *Volantix* lay jumbled on the galley floor, wet and cold, freezing in the absolute dark.

And Tom remembered Jenny's words, that he might find his doom in the icy North and never find his way back to be her friend at all.

THEN AS THEY LAY IN THE BLACKNESS, feeling the ship shudder, the wind veered. It began to skirt over different edges in the great cliff of ice above them, and the noise it made turned to evil shrieking. And no one moved or said anything until the two sailors in the corner began to sob.

"The cold winds with ghost voices!" they cried.

The Voyage North

CHAPTER FOUR:
THE FIRST MATE'S STORY

THEN AS THEY LAY THERE IN THE NIGHT WITH the wind shrieking and the ship shuddering and the sea twisting and slewing the *Volantix* on its anchors, Tom thought of what Jenny would say about him. *"For being content to lie wet and freezing and bereft of light is not,"* he could hear her say, *"what I call being resourceful in misadventure."* For a moment, Tom wished with all his heart that she really was there, to say it herself. And then he pulled out the tinderbox Jenny had given him and struck a spark.

In the light of the little ember Tom could just see the faces of all of the sailors peering out of the darkness towards him as though they had been awakened from a bad dream.

One of the sailors passed Tom a lantern and he lit that. "Good work, lads," the Captain said, still white from the ice and storm, staggering up to his feet. "Now get that stove going, for it's dreadful cold."

The First Mate began counting to make sure all hands were present while Tom and the Cook and the two sailors in the corner all set to relighting the stove. Some of the others went looking for the bucklers that covered the portholes and started wedging them back tight with mallets and slivers of wood.

Soon the stove was roaring and the hold was all sealed up snug. It was still dark, and the storm still blew and tossed the *Volantix* up and down, but the shivering sailors gathered around the fire in the big galley stove began to feel a little warmer and drier. The Cook took the chance to go to the manger and comfort his nanny goat. "Not that it won't happen again," he told her.

"Perhaps you'd all like to hear how I got my parrot," the First Mate said, as he changed his neckcloth for a dry one.

There was silence all around, but then the Captain said, "That sounds like a story that might warm us up. Go right ahead."

"IT WAS FAR TO THE EAST," the First Mate began:

"It was as far to the East and South as we're going to the West and North, though I guess that when you go West as far as we're going, you come to the East, and vicey-versey, though the other way, it's a much warmer trip."

"Less ice, but more lizards, I hear," one of the sailors said.

"Longer around, but less time shivering," one of the sailors said.

"Sun so warm you browns like a muffin!" a third one cried.

"Sultry winds that lick your face!"

The Voyage North

"Air so hot –"

"All very true," the First Mate cut in, "but who's been there, you or me, and who has the parrot to prove it?

"So anyway," he went on, "it was far to the East, where the fish are like bright gems that dance in the crown of the sea. And some of them fly in the air over your ship and if you bring a racquet you can use them to play badminton, and then when you're done lob them right into the pot for dinner.

"It's true.

"And some of them are shaped like blobs but have a hundred wormy arms that they'll hug you down into the water with, and then no one knows what happens to you, except some say you grow gills and live like a prince in the kingdom of the sea, and some say you just get et.

"And all of the people in those parts are tanned dark all year round, and even in their great cities they speak in strange words, though they say ours sound just as strange to them.

"But I was navigator on a queer Eastern ship with two great sails that spread like bat wings; and we took ivory tusks and snuff boxes from Zunna-wundoor to Wan-daling, and then took jade masks with three eyes, and a kind of tea that makes your ears turn blue, all the way back from Wan-daling to Zunna-wundoor.

"And one day a typhoon found us, and we spoomed before it until we were blown off our charts and into a place in the Spice Islands where it was so warm the people wore nothing but shells and flowers and grass skirts, and spoke a lingo that none of us could make out – not even our helmsman, Ziff-ling McRanga-wux, who could speak almost anything, on account of his unusual parentage...."

And while the First Mate spoke, it was a curious thing, but the Captain and Tom and all the crew, even the two sailors in the corner, listened so hard they almost began to feel they were there too, on a lazy island that bloomed like a summer flower, as if they had already shouldered through the icy narrows and dropped down the other side of the West into spice winds and warm waters, and the storm that still battered at the bucklers on the portholes was already a long ago memory – just a story they told at evenings by the fire.

"But we needed to speak to the islanders somehow," the First Mate was explaining, "for in the stormy confusion of the typhoon we had lost many supplies and provisions."

"Barrels of fresh water," suggested one sailor.

"Yes," said the First Mate, "we needed barrels of water and new rope."

"More salt meat and sea biscuits," suggested another sailor."

"Yes," said the First Mate, "we needed more food and new maps, for we were lost."

"Lantern oil?" a third sailor guessed.

"Yes," said the First Mate, "we needed more lantern oil, for we had lost almost everything, and most of all we

The Voyage North

needed a great tree to serve as a mainmast, for ours had broken in the gale. So," he added, before anyone could speak again, "we needed to speak to the islanders, but we didn't know their talk, nor they ours.

"We just stood and smiled at them in their feathers and shells and felt the sweat running down our backs."

"Did you try speaking very slowly?" one of the sailors asked.

The First Mate glared. "Tried it."

"Did you attempt writing down what you meant," the Cook, who was literate, asked.

The First Mate stared at him balefully. "Yes, but seeing as how they couldn't make us out when we talked, so it turned out that somehow they couldn't read our writing either. But we tried it."

"Did you try to communicate by making signs?" the Captain asked.

The First Mate looked at him sadly. "Yes, sir, we made the attempt," he said, "but we found our vocabulary insufficient to our needs." Then he pulled off his fresh neckcloth in frustration. "But who's telling this story, you all or me, and who has the tattoo to prove he was there?" he demanded.

"A tattoo?" said Tom.

"Yes," said the First Mate, "for they're the ones who invented the art and in fact they gave me a complimentary one, but that comes later in the story, if you'll all stop interrupting." And he pulled up his thick sweater and then his striped jersey.

Everyone leaned close to stare, for there on the First Mate's belly was a very impressive tattoo indeed, an enormous roaring tiger, drawn in blue beneath his skin, but they didn't dare interrupt again or say anything about it. They just opened their eyes wide and listened harder.

The First Mate pulled down his jersey and went on: "So after an interval of nodding and bowing and smiling and making signs with our hands in the hot sun, and all the bowing making us sweat and making their shells tinkle," he said, "they were as hospitable as anyone could be, considering they didn't know if we were really trying to speak to them or just were a boatload of waterlogged wretches with their wits pickled by the briny sea.

"But they gave us necklaces of fresh flowers to wear, just as if we were honoured guests, and brought us gourds of cool water to drink, and served us a tasty kind of fish with five eyes and oysters that had shells that sparkled with diamonds, and then for dessert coconut milk and fruits we'd never seen before, even in Wan-daling or Zunna-wundoor."

"Like *bergamots* you mean?" said the Cook, who had travelled a bit himself.

"Stranger than bergamots," said the First Mate. "Fruits that grew in great violet bunches and tasted like cherries and pears together, and fruits that was shaped like stars and tasted like sweet wine. And we ate it all while they just stared at us piteously like we were poor idiot half-drowned fools, which I suppose we were.

N

39

The Voyage North

"So I took it on me to go wandering over the island, looking for what we needed myself, and I found a sapphire pool with a lovely young woman bathing, but that wasn't what we wanted, and I found a palm tree where monkeys had made a cuckoo clock, but that wasn't what we wanted, and I found many another thing which is written up in no book we know, but none of them were what we wanted.

"And when I was tired of walking and not finding the right things, I lay down under the strange Southern stars, wishing there were only some way to learn the islanders' strange speech and ask for what we wanted, and fell asleep."

The First Mate paused then, and looked all around, and Tom could tell he was just daring any of them to interrupt again. "And when I woke up," the First Mate said, "it was morning and that's when I saw this parrot staring down at me from a palm tree and singing, *'Ding-dong, that's my song, Ding-dong, sailors up and move along.'*"

He lifted up his parrot proudly. "Ding-dong!" the parrot said.

"I don't know where he learned *our* speech," the First Mate said, "but these birds live an awful long time, and he knew it from somewhere, and he knew how the islanders talked too, and so he taught me enough of their lingo to get by on, sitting there under the palm tree. And the last word he taught me was *Koway-roway-raro!*'"

At that, the First Mate's parrot began to screech. *"Koway-roway-raro! Koway-roway-raro!"* it cried. "Tiger!

Tiger! Awk! Run! *Koway-roway-raro!* Run you lubbers! Awk!"

"Just so," said the First Mate, patting his parrot to calm it down, "for there *was* a tiger!"

The Captain put down his pipe and Tom and all the crew leaned in closer.

"So we ran, me carrying the parrot, like a three-masted schooner racing for harbour ahead of a gale," the First Mate said, "through the palm trees and past the pools of sapphire-blue water and on and on till we was right back in the middle of the islanders' village, where I fell down gasping.

"And there they stood, the crew from our sloop and all the islanders in their shells and feathers and blue tattoos, all staring at me while I was panting to get my breath back, like I was mad as two cats in a fountain. Then I said, 'Tiger, I saw a tiger,' and all our crew laughed, and then I said *'Koway-roway-raro,'* and all of the islanders laughed and clapped and shook their shells with pleasure to hear me speaking in their own tongue.

"Ziff-ling, he was miffed at first that I could speak a talk he couldn't, but the parrot taught him too soon enough, and the islanders was tickled to talk with anyone dressed as odd as we and helped us with all the provisioning we could ask for."

The First Mate took a deep breath, for he was not used to speaking so long without interruption, and then he finished, "And in honour of our first conversation, they gave me this tattoo, and that's why it's a tiger."

N

41

The Voyage North

"You outran a tiger?" Tom said. "Aren't they awfully fast?"

"Quick on the pounce," the First Mate said, casually. "But no wind for distance if they don't catch you first thing."

TOM AND THE CAPTAIN and the whole crew, even the two sailors in the corner, were quiet a moment, still thinking about the spice islands and the tanned people dressed all in shells and feathers and flowers, and the First Mate's parrot and the adventure with the Tiger, and wondering about getting tattoos themselves, and still forgetting about the fearsome storm that battered and rocked the *Volantix*.

And then the Captain spoke. "Mate," he said, "we may be stormbound for some days. Why don't you teach us all some of the island language your parrot taught you, to pass the time?"

"Fair enough," the First Mate said, drinking some hot chocolate the Cook had passed around in tin cups. "Well, repeat after me then. To say hello, you go, '*Oola-woola-woona-hei*.'"

"*Oola-woola-woona-hei*," repeated Tom and all the crew.

"And to ask if someone wants a cracker, you go, '*Woola-honey-boola-woola?*'"

"*Woola-honey-boola-woola?*" they all said after him.

42

The sailors looked around in wonder

CHAPTER FIVE:
THE NARROWING WAY

A FTER THREE NIGHTS OF THE STORM, OF HEARING its terrible screams and the moans of the ship as it bumped and ground against the ice, the crew woke up to feel the *Volantix* resting calm in the icy sea. It took three sailors putting their backs against the hatch to crack the crust of snow and frost and heave it open.

Then as the fresh cold air poured down into the ship, Tom looked up into the sky and saw that it was clear. It was still dark, for the nights were long now, and not done by morning, but there was a hint of blue from the dawn to come, and he knew the storm was over.

The sailors, frowzy from three days confined in the hold, rushed up onto the open deck, held their lanterns high, and looked around in wonder.

"MY POOR BARKY," the First Mate said at last (for when sailors are fond of a ship they call it a *barky*).

The *Volantix* might have been the ghost of the ship they knew, for it was all changed to white. Every line hung low, bearded with ice, and every part of the ship – deck, spars, rope, rail, and the furled sails hung from the yards – was deep with snow that glistened in the lantern light.

The crew set to clearing the decks as fast as they could, and in the shining darkness the sailors ran along the lines and laughed at the crack and smash they made as they kicked off the icicles.

Except for the two sailors who tried to make their way back to the poop deck, walking slowly and carefully. "Oh no –" cried the first one, as he lost his balance and slid back across the icy poop deck and bumped down the starboard ladder.

"It's slippery –" cried the second one, as he lost his balance and slid across the icy poop deck and bumped down the port ladder.

And, "Whoaa!" they both cried as they slid on, even faster now, past Tom on either side, and down the length of the ship. As so they kept on, spinning on their backs like curling rocks, following the curve of the sides, until they met at the bow and knocked themselves onto their feet again.

No one watching could keep from laughing, but the crew cheered and applauded their spectacular recovery. "Are you all right?" Tom called.

"Yes," the two sailors said, as they slowly started back to the poop deck, holding on to one another for support and trying to keep some dignity.

"We meant to do that," one of them explained.

"We've been practicing," the other one added.

46

Then everyone began laughing again. They laughed till they were gasping in the fresh cold air, overjoyed to be alive and outside again.

"Of course," said the Cook at last, wiping the frozen tears from his eyes, "we're all still doomed." Which only started the crew laughing once more.

But around them the sea was all changed from the storm.

WHILE THE CAPTAIN AND THE FIRST MATE frowned over their charts and instruments by the binnacle on the poop deck, Tom carefully crept up the frozen shrouds to the crow's nest to have a look aloft. "What do you see, Tom?" the First Mate called.

"*Ice!*" Tom cried, miserably. "Before there was ice in the sea, but now there's only slivers of sea running through the ice!"

"We moved in the storm, even though anchored to this iceberg," the Captain said. "For the iceberg itself is only a giant vessel of the sea, and sailed with the wind and waves. So we're West of where we started, and that's good, for that's where we mean to go, but we're North too, and that's put us in more ice."

"And no wind now at all," the First Mate said. Then to the rest of the crew, who'd been trying to pretend they weren't listening, he said, "So leave the sheets and rigging all you sailors, and fish the anchors and unship the oars!"

The Voyage North

Soon the crew had pulled the anchors from the sea and put their mittens to the long sweeps that were the *Volantix*'s great oars. "Pull hard!" the Captain cried. And they pulled hard indeed, and so moved the ship slowly out of their frozen cove and down the widest of the rivers that were all that was left for passage through the ice.

They pulled mighty hard, and everyone took their turn, even young Tom and the Captain, for they all could see that this water too was freezing fast, and soon they might be frozen with it.

When the water had grown too narrow to ply the sweeps, the Captain ordered the sailors over the side. "We'll have to drag her now," he said, "haul along this icy shore like barge donkeys and drag the *Volantix* through the narrow water behind us."

So they moved the ship, by rope and main force. It was desperate work, and cold, and sometimes sailors half-plunged through the ice before their fellows could pull them out and send them aboard with chattering teeth to warm up by the stove. And as they hauled, they sang slowly:

> *Heave, ho! it's West we go,*
> *Through the Eaves of the World and the icy Xow!*
> *Heave, to! and make it through,*
> *Till we Wnd the home of the cockatoo!*
> *Heave, haul! and it's one for all,*
> *And cry woe betide should the goblins call!*

N

48

Heave, lads, haul, Tom,
Till the ropes are straining!
Haul, lads, heave, Tom,
For the warm West waiting!

Heave, ho! it's West we go,
Through the Eaves of the World and the icy Xow!
Haul, heave! it's South we seek,
Where the spice winds blow and trees are teak!
But now heave, ho! for it's North we know,
The Eaves of the World and the icy Xow.

They pulled the *Volantix* behind them, west along the salt river that ran through the ice, pulling and pulling and never stopping, for the water grew narrower by the hour. They pulled until they thought they could pull no longer, and then they still went on, and Tom pulled until he fell on the ice, too exhausted to get back on his feet.

The Captain called a halt and bent over him. "Tom, young Tom," the Captain said, "I'm sorry I wasn't watching you better. You're our guide and Kalifax, and we need you well." He helped Tom up.

"I'm sorry," Tom said, "I can pull again."

"No, lad," the First Mate said, "we need you on the ship. Have something to eat and warm up by the stove, then keep watch from the bowsprit."

So the Captain ordered too, and the crew pulled on without Tom. Once he had recovered, Tom crept along the

The Voyage North

twisting spar at the front of the ship and sat with his legs
dangling over water and looked ahead for any trouble.

The crew had hauled right through the short day, and
the evening light had come again, so Tom lit the great
lantern that hung over the bow. In its light he could see
the ice closing in even more, until they only made way by
using the iron cutwater on the prow of the *Volantix* to
drive through the narrow river like a wedge.

The night came and the moon rose, and every hour
the ship crept slower and the crew pulled harder and
stumbled more often. Finally it seemed the *Volantix* had
stopped moving through the darkening seas altogether.

But it was just then that Tom sat up straight and cried:
"Open water! The moonlight shows open water to the
West! Pull, pull, pull! For it's only a hundred yards more!
Oh, pull hard for open water!"

"Pull!" called the Captain.

"Pull!" called the First Mate. "Pull all, pull! Pull for
your lives but *pull!"*

And the crew of the *Volantix* pulled. They pulled until
the ropes hummed, they heaved until the lines were so
tight you could have played them like a fiddle, and they
strained until, with a great squeak and crack, the cords
unravelled and snapped apart, and all the sailors tumbled
forward and onto the ice in a heap.

But the *Volantix* hadn't moved another inch.

"Oh!" cried Tom, *"Oh!* A hundred yards to open water,
just a hundred yards! What will we do?"

The Voyage North

But the Captain was already back on his boots and he didn't wait an instant. "Hitch those ropes together!" he commanded, "for we're not done pulling yet. And the gun crew with me to the foredeck, for now we'll try our smasher."

So the Captain and four of the sailors climbed up and began aiming the great short cannon on the foredeck to point down into the ice right ahead of the *Volantix*. While they worked, Tom scrambled down into the hold for extra bags of gunpowder.

Just as Tom got back above deck, the gun crew lit the fuse and everyone clapped their hands over their ears and bent away.

The smasher went off with a bang that made the whole ship – and even the ice under the sailors still at the tow ropes – shudder. The huge cannonball crashed into the ice just forward of the *Volantix* and broke through into the sea below, sending up great frozen shards and a shower of sea water, while the cannon jumped back on its wheels and rolled to the edge of the fore deck.

The sailors on the ice cheered, and the Captain cried "Reload! A few more shots like that and we might sail free!"

Tom passed ahead a bag of gunpowder and looked around, dizzy with excitement, and half-blinded by the flash of the cannon in the night. All along the Northern horizon green and blue lights were rising up, and for a moment Tom thought the blast from the smasher might have woken some sleeping stars and started them rising up to the Roof of the World.

But then Tom looked again, and it seemed to his dazzled eyes that the lights weren't so much rising as creeping closer. That didn't seem right, and he looked at the Captain and the gun crew, but they were all intent on their next shot, sponging out the barrel and ramming home the new ball.

And as his eyes cleared, Tom looked out at the lights again, green and blue and creeping closer, and then he went and shook the Captain's sleeve and pointed, and the Captain stopped straightaway. For he knew what those lights meant: they were the snow-goblins, holding their *glims,* the icy lanterns that shine green and blue, and his heart went cold.

Now the whole crew could see the silhouettes of the small dark shapes. Dark shapes with twisted helmets and small thin axes.

"Goblinry," the Cook said glumly. "More or less what I've been expecting."

And "Goblinry!" the Captain cried to the sailors on the ice. "All aboard, for it's goblinry! Never mind the ropes, but all on deck and find your swords!"

IF ICY COLD HAD TEETH and claws and small thin axes it would be like the snow-goblins. And if a wolf had the patience of winter and the bottomless hunger of the seas

The Voyage North

and the cunning, cruel frozen heart of a nightmare, it would be like the snow-goblins. But as it is, nothing that lives and walks the earth is as half so bad – except the ice trolls who are stupid rather than cunning, but larger and otherwise just as wicked.

So now the snow-goblins ran carefully and silently towards the *Volantix*. Carefully, for they had three plans to seize this prize, and it had been many ages since they had captured a ship of mortal sailors. Silently, because they never made any noise in any case, never at all, no more than the falling snow.

If the battle they fought for the *Volantix* that night is seldom remembered by men and women, the snow-goblins mark it every year, and for now you will have to guess whether the memory makes them smile, or gnash their teeth in bitterness. And mortal children mark it too, for that's the night they play at monsters come calling.

The goblins' first plan was simple enough: close with the ship, board the ship, slay the ship's sailors. And the closer they came, the more they hungered and the faster they ran, for they could smell the sailors, and to goblins, the sailors smelled like meat.

Soon the goblins were close enough to see the sailors too, and the sailors were ready on the deck of the *Volantix*, swords drawn.

But that never daunted the goblins, for it had been many ages since they had enjoyed a shipful of mortal sailors, and they were hungry.

N

The Voyage North

It was then that the Captain ordered all the starboard guns be fired together – a broadside – and the night roared with flame and thunder.

But the goblins expected that, and anyway, most of the cannonballs only struck the ice and sent up shards of frozen sea that could do them no harm, for they were snow-goblins. Still, some of the balls hit home and rolled through several ranks, crushing the goblins in their path and making those that were near scramble away, for the touch of iron is deadly to such creatures. But the goblins who were struck simply melted into water with an angry hiss, and were taken back into the icy water where they had been born.

Then the goblins were alongside the *Volantix*, and right beneath the barrels of her guns. They thought they were safe, for the cannons couldn't fire straight down at them, and for the first time they made a noise. The noise was the sound of their thin axes as the goblins swung them and they struck home into the timbers of the *Volantix*.

And so the goblins pulled themselves up and aboard.

"REPEL BOARDERS!" the First Mate cried, "defy the frozen monsters!" He looked at the two sailors on the poop deck, who were more frightened than usual, and added, for their benefit, "And *woe betide* the snow-goblins!"

"Woe betide the snow-goblins!" all the sailors yelled, and they took it as their battle cry.

"*Woe!*" cried the Captain as he drew his pistol and shot

down the first goblin who dared to raise his head above the bulwark, and *"Woe!"* cried all the sailors as they joined their swords to the fray, and *"Woe!"* cried Tom from the port rail, where the Captain had ordered him to stay safe.

And for a long time the sailors and goblins fought, swords ringing off twisted helmets and clashing against thin axes. And from the sound of it you would have thought the sailors were having the worst of it, for when one of them got cut their skin froze around the wound straightaway and they yelled hard, but when their steel swords bit into a goblin's flesh, the little monster just melted away with an angry hiss.

BUT IN TRUTH the sailors had the height of the ship on their side, and their steel swords could cleave a goblin's helmet through if they swung them hard, and slowly they beat the goblins back by the light of the setting moon, and were almost ready to cry victory.

The Voyage North

The snow-goblins set to work on their second plan

CHAPTER SIX:
THE BATTLE ON
THE FROZEN SEA

S O THE GOBLINS WHO HAD PULLED THEMSELVES
aboard were a silent horror to the sailors, and to Tom,
who hid himself by the port rail. The First Mate himself
had fallen to the deck, from having his wooden leg cut in
half, though he was otherwise all right.

But in their hunger the snow-goblins had forgotten
how hard the steel of mortals bit. Already, many a goblin
had been slain, and turned to ice water that ran over the
decks, through the scuppers, and back into the sea.

SO EVEN AS THE BATTLE ON DECK began to turn
against them, the snow-goblins set to work on their second plan. For a whole company of goblins had held back
on the ice by the stern of the *Volantix*. Now this rearguard
took their thin axes to the ship and began to chop a hole
in her checkered side. They meant to crawl into the hold
while the battle still raged on deck, and so catch the crew
by surprise from below.

But when the First Mate hopped back towards the
stern to take a moment from the battle and fit on his spare

peg, the parrot happened to look down at the ice and spot the goblins at work on their second plan. His red crest quivered.

"Awk!" the parrot shrieked, into the First Mate's ear. "Awk! Goblins! Help, you lubbers!" and then, slipping back into his island speech, *"Gobo-loona-rissa-rei!"*

"What?" cried the First Mate – *"Gobo-loona!"* Then he saw them himself and didn't hesitate. "Coals!" he yelled, "hot coals from the stove!" But in the midst of the battle, only the Cook heard him.

"The sort of thing I knew would happen; they'll get the poor nanny goat, and then the rest of us, and we'll all get et like ice sherbet," the Cook muttered, but he hopped briskly down into the galley nonetheless and passed up a scuttle full of burning coals. The First Mate took it, and with his new leg on securely, ran back to the stern, where he flung the coals down at the monsters below. Wherever they struck, a goblin melted, and the First Mate hurried back. "Let's have more!" he called to the Cook, "for it liquefies 'em most efficiently."

As Tom hid, and the other sailors fought the goblins with swords, the Cook and the First Mate between them made a relay of trading hot coals for empty scuttles.

So the goblins' second plan to gain the ship melted away by the stern of the *Volantix*. Only one of the monsters ever squeezed through the hole they made and into the ship's hold, but the nanny goat butted him flat and then the Cook finished him off with a hot poker. "Good work, girlie," the Cook told the goat, patting her head. "Though it's only staving off the inevitable, you poor doomed beastie."

MEANWHILE, the Captain was fencing with the last of the snow-goblins who'd dared the side. The goblin swung low, but the Captain jumped over the axe, struck the monster backhand with the pommel of his sword, and then ran it through. As the goblin melted away (just when the low moon disappeared at last) the whole crew cheered for victory.

Down on the dark ice below there were still some goblins gathered under the starboard side of the *Volantix*, but scattered all around them, wherever a goblin had fallen, were dozens of the strange, cold goblin-glims, still shining blue and green.

As the sailors stared down through the darkness at them, the goblins began to edge backwards. But the joy of battle was in the crew, and the Captain had no wish to be surprised by the same goblins a second time.

"Over the sides and after them, those who can!" the Captain called, and the crew swung down over the rail and chased across the ice and after the monsters, shouting, *"Woe! Woe!* Woe from the *Volantix!"* until Tom and the wounded sailors lost sight of them in the frozen night.

The Voyage North

THAT WAS HOW THE GOBLINS' FIRST PLAN, to board
the side of the *Volantix* from the North, failed, and you
have heard about how the First Mate and the Cook
spoiled their second plan, to chop a hole in the good ship's
side and enter her from below.

But the goblins had laid three plans, and the third didn't
begin until the Captain and all the unwounded sailors
were chasing what remained of the first band of monsters
North over the dark arctic ice.

A troop of the tallest, coldest goblins had been sent to
carefully creep wide around the stern of the *Volantix*.
They had kept the shutters on their cold goblin-glims
closed so they showed no light, and of course they made
no sound ever, no more than the falling snow. None of the
sailors had seen them come or knew how close they were.

By the time the Captain and most of the crew disappeared North into the night, hunting the remains of the
first band of goblins and cutting them down with relish,
this last troop of snow-goblins (the tallest and coldest)
crouched undetected on the South side of the *Volantix*.

Now they rose in the darkness and swung their grap-
pling hooks and began to pull themselves quietly up the
side of the ship.

The nanny goat bleated and bleated again in terror.
But none of the sailors left on board, who were mostly
hurt and tired anyway, understood her, or knew they were
under attack again.

Not until Tom happened to look round from the port

guardrail, where he'd been crouching. Suddenly Tom found himself staring right into the face of the tallest, coldest, quietest goblin of them all, who was just about to swing his leg onto the deck.

Tom didn't have a moment to think. He grabbed a stout iron belaying pin and brought it down so hard he cracked the goblin's head – helmet, skull, and all. The monster melted away into the darkness below with a hiss of angry water.

"Broadside!" Tom yelled desperately. The heads of other goblins were already appearing at the rail to take their leader's place. "Fire a port broadside!" Tom cried again.

Then Tom did have a moment to think, and he saw doom by cold and goblinry all about him, just as Jenny had prophesied. And Tom became very scared.

OUT ON THE ICE, the Captain and the sailors had to give up their chase at last.

Many a goblin had hissed in fury to be struck down and melted away, but the few who were left were snow-goblins still, and could make better time running over the tumbled ice than the exhausted sailors, not a few of whom had taken wounds in the pursuit.

So they stopped, and the Captain called them into order, and they stood, panting and looking around, wondering how to find their way back to the *Volantix*, lost in the darkness behind them. Several sailors had taken goblin-glims as trophies, and they held them up for light, but no matter how far they looked, they only saw ice.

And because they had run far and fought hard, they were damp with sweat and starting to shiver in the cold. The Captain pulled out his star-glass and held it up to work out what way to start back, but just then a great flash of flame burst through the black night and they all held their breaths.

When they finally heard the boom of cannons roll over the ice, they knew what the flame had been, and that it marked where their ship must lie.

"It's the cannons of the *Volantix!*" the First Mate cried. "It's a ragged broadside, but they've fired all guns!"

The Captain put his glass back in his pocket. "One more run lads!" he called. "The goblins must be attacking her from portside, and there's only wounded sailors and young Tom left aboard! *Run!*"

"*Run!*" all the sailors shouted as they began to pound over the ice again, "Run to save the ship!" And they ran, and, when they could, they shouted, "*Woe!*"

ON BOARD THE *Volantix* the wounded sailors had just managed to fire the port guns before most of the goblins swung over the rails. The cannonballs had taken care of several of the largest monsters, and some of the others had been so close to the mouths of the guns that they had just melted away from the heat of the blast.

But still a half-dozen of the tallest snow-goblins survived the broadside to climb aboard. So the wounded sailors fought the last and most terrible battle, swords against axes, on the deck of the *Volantix*. The thin axes of the goblins bit cruelly, and not a few of the sailors screamed as they were hurt again.

As for Tom, he was scared and scunnered and unarmed, for he had dropped the belaying pin, which was his only weapon, and tried to shrink himself as small and inconspicuous as he could. While the sailors fought the goblins, Tom only crouched against the gunwales and shook with fear.

You might wonder at that, for Tom had already watched one battle with the goblins on the deck of the *Volantix*, and had just struck down the tallest goblin of them all himself. But now Tom learned that nightmares are worse the second time, and dangers more terrible if you have time to think.

"Not an heroic posture," he knew Jenny would say. *"Nor stout-hearted and deWant, which all tales account mighty Explorers to be."* Still, Tom trembled as the battle wore on; but the sailors handled their sabres and cutlasses with desperate courage, and they cried *"Woe!"* and woe befell the snow-goblins, until there was but one left and he turned and ran, swinging his axe all around him and heading straight for Tom.

Whether the goblin meant to strike him down, or simply jump over the side, Tom never knew. Just as the whirling axe was over Tom's head, one of the sailors cast a harpoon at the monster's back.

The goblin stopped short, pierced by iron. As he melted with an angry hiss the harpoon dropped point down to lodge itself in the deck, with the goblin's twisted helmet wobbling round the end. But the goblin's thin axe dropped too, and as it fell, it nicked Tom's forehead.

Then for a moment the icy water that was all that was left of the monster pooled around Tom before pouring over the side. And for the rest of his days, Tom remembered the cold fear of the water's touch.

Now the sailors on the *Volantix*, hurt and exhausted, looked North again, and wondered what had happened in the chase on the ice. They saw blue and green lanterns coming towards them, and at first they feared their friends had all been lost and the goblins were coming back.

And out on the ice, the sailors with the Captain were wondering if their friends on the ship had been lost too. So they ran on and on until they saw the glow of the ship's own great yellow lanterns, two astern and one ahead, and the Captain yelled up from the ice, *"Volantix*, my ship, my crew, what news?"

And Tom wept with relief to hear the Captain's voice, and dropped a line down, and soon the whole crew of the *Volantix* were gathered together again. Tom himself now had a great bandage on his forehead where the last goblin's axe had struck, and the others made much of him, especially the Captain, who said, "Tom, you are our Kalifax, for we'd have lost our ship without your alarm."

The Cook seemed out of sorts for having survived, but he joined all the other sailors as they danced around Tom, rejoicing in their victory over the snow-goblins. Even the two sailors on the poop deck, who said they'd never been afraid. But Tom never forgot that *he* had.

WHEN THE FIRST MATE broke off from dancing his second celebratory hornpipe, he looked over the bow and remembered the *Volantix* needed to break free of the ice and make for the open sea. Somehow it seemed to him the ice had become thicker during the battle, and closed in so there was hardly any way forward.

And indeed it had, for as they were slain the snow-goblins had played a final trick. When they melted they ran into the sea ahead of the *Volantix* and there they froze at once into terrible ice, thick and goblin-cursed.

When the Captain realized what had happened, he ordered the smasher filled. They fired into the ice beneath the prow of the *Volantix*, not once, but a dozen times. Over and over as quick as they could, till the barrel of the great gun was red-hot.

Every time one of the smasher's balls, each as heavy as Tom, struck the ice, a great shower of frost went up, but the cannon never broke through to the sea, no matter how often they fired. The goblin ice just froze around the ship even thicker. Finally the Captain called a ceasefire, and the gun crew lay gasping about the deck of the *Volantix*. Tom sobbed with frustration.

For they had weathered the storm, and manned the sweeps to move down the river in the ice, and then hauled the ship by main force. And just when it looked like they might find open water, they'd had to beat back three attacks by the goblins – and not lost a single sailor – and then launched a dozen blasts at the frozen sea.

But for all that they were stuck, locked solid, marooned in the ice, and had no prospect of release.

So the Captain spoke: "Tom and all you sailors," he said, "you've rowed, hauled, fought, and worked the guns harder than any crew has ever done in a single day, but we've had bad luck and it looks like winter's caught us." And then he stopped, for he had heard a faint noise in the night, and he looked up.

THE LOW MOON WAS LONG GONE NOW, but the whole black sky was alight. There were fans of blue and white, and tongues of violet and green, all twisting together, and it seemed that far off in the great icy stillness they could hear the hiss and crackle of mighty flames.

"*Fire!*" cried Tom, suddenly wild with happiness. "*Fire that dances in the black night sky!*"

The Voyage North

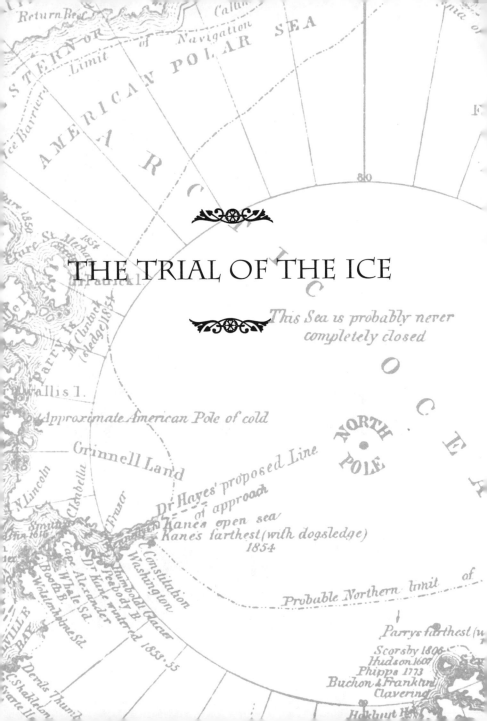

THE TRIAL OF THE ICE

The sailors set a wide perimeter of green and blue glims

CHAPTER SEVEN:
MAROONED

So THE *Volantix* LAY MAROONED IN THE DARKNESS, for the battle with the snow-goblins had marked the fall of the Long Night, and the sun would never rise again that year.

And if the Queen of the Hall of the Stars had chanced to look down from her velvet throne, she would have seen it all, laid out like a painting – just as Tom did whenever he climbed to his old post in the crow's nest.

There in the middle of the deep black night lay the *Volantix*, every part of it rimed and hung with icicles. It was listing to port, and its checkered hull showed dark against the pale gloom of the frozen sea. Around the ship the sailors had set a wide perimeter of green and blue glims, the goblin lanterns that never burn out, so that no one would wander too far away into the icy dark and be lost.

At the bow, one of the ship's own lanterns cast a great circle of light, and there were two of them at the stern, and her cabin windows glowed yellow.

THEY WERE FROZEN SNUG, and when the deep currents

in the sea below moved, the ice boomed and cracked and screamed and the joints of the *Volantix* moaned in its grasp. All around the ship the sailors moved among the lights, keeping busy, but there were always a few who stopped to look up at the flames that danced among the stars and made the great frozen vistas around them glow and change.

"Don't despair," the Captain had told them, "for though we are now in great danger, the First Mate and I laid plans in case it came to this. And the fire in the sky is one of the wonders we came to see, and surely its lighting now, when all seems grim, is a sign of hope."

So the sailors took heart when they looked up, and even when the flames died low, there were the stars themselves. Of course, all sailors know the stars, and know the shapes they make: the Hunter, and the Cross, and the Great Bear which guards the North Star. But now they were in the Eaves of the World, almost at the rafters of the sky, and all the stars shone nearer and brighter than any mortal man or woman had ever seen.

To Tom, in the crow's nest, they seemed almost near enough to touch.

AFTER THE BATTLE ON THE FROZEN SEA, the Captain and the First Mate retired to go over their plans, and while they spoke together the crew waited, and discussed their plight themselves. Some thought they were safer for having fought off the goblins, and others thought there would only be more to come.

"No, we survived the schemes of the snow-goblins," the Cook said. "But wait until the ice trolls, who are stupid rather than cunning, but larger and otherwise just as wicked."

"*The ice trolls!*" wailed the two sailors on the poop deck. "Do they eat people too?"

"They eat trollibags, exclusively," said the Cook.

Then Tom felt a wave of relief. "And what are trollibags?" Tom asked.

"Insides," said the parrot.

"Insides?" Tom asked.

"In this case, people's insides," the Cook said.

But the Captain and the First Mate had stepped out in time to hear the end of the discussion, and while the First Mate only shook his head at the Cook's words, for once the Captain grew angry with his sailors.

"*Belay such talk!*" the Captain called. "The *Volantix* is not cursed, nor doomed, nor ill-starred, but the luckiest ship ever to sail, with the stoutest crew, who'd make short work of any troll, goblin, lurrikin or other fell creature that dared to cross us!"

"Yes, sir," said the Cook, abashed.

But the two sailors only whimpered. "*Trollibags!* We'll be trollibags!"

"Never mind that," the Captain said. "Think of what's inside the ice trolls." Tom, the Cook, the two sailors, and

The Trial of the Ice

all the rest of the crew leaned close to hear. "Tell them," the Captain said to the First Mate.

"Slush and snowballs, I've heard tell," the First Mate said, right away. "Nothing to 'em, really. Now let's attend to business."

And then for a long time the sailors were too busy to worry.

"FIRST THINGS FIRST!" the First Mate had cried, and so he set the crew to work plugging the hole the goblins had chopped in the *Volantix's* side, a hole only large enough for a goblin to crawl through.

"But if we ever get out of the ice," the First Mate pointed out, "it will founder us in a minute."

Then, once they were done that, "Second things second," the First Mate said. "We'll pile the icy monsters' helmets in a great cairn to warn them against trying their luck attacking the *Volantix* again."

So the sailors gathered the twisted black helmets and carried them as far North as they could, without losing sight of the ship, and heaped them together.

(But here they needn't have worried, for all the snow-goblins that remained for hundreds of miles around were hiding in their caves, and gnashed their teeth with bitterness.)

The third piece of business was trickier. For the Captain and the First Mate were worried that as winter wore on and the ice stretched and shrank with the flow of the sea far beneath, the seams of the *Volantix* might be crushed in its grasp.

"Here's our third job," the Captain told the crew after he and the First Mate had settled on what to do, "and it's the hardest so far. We'll never get the *Volantix* to open water this winter, for the ice stretches farther West each day. And we might be able to drag one of the ship's boats and catch the last of the open water, but what then?"

"What then?" the First Mate said after him, "for our largest boat would never hold more than ten sailors, and nowhere near enough provisions to see them through to the other side of the West."

"But," the Captain said, "if we could lift the *Volantix* from the ice, the First Mate thinks we might be able to rig great runners and drag her like a sledge. It would be tremendous hard work, but in time we could make it back to the iceberg where we weathered the storm and find some better shelter in one of its coves. And the ice could never crush us, for we'd sit above it."

So the sailors went to work right away sharp. They gathered all the wood they thought they could spare and set huge bonfires burning alongside the ship to soften the ice. Then they got out the mighty timbers the *Volantix* carried in case the masts or the yards had to be replaced, and jammed them between the starboard hull and the ice. Then half the crew pulled down hard on the timbers to lever the ship *up,* while from the other side the rest (including Tom) tugged on ropes from the other side to pull the ship *out*.

But perhaps it was still cursed by the goblins, for the ice never let the *Volantix* go, no matter how hard they pulled and strained. So all the planning and all the firewood and spare timbers, and all the hauling and levering came to nothing, except that the sailors kept busy in the cold and they broke two spars and snapped several ropes.

The First Mate fell to muttering many things, and his parrot after him, and then they took turns and swore and cursed and imprecated in a stream of scurrility and execrations as only sailors and parrots of vast experience can, but in the end they had to admit his plan had failed.

That left only the fourth piece of business to try.

74

AND THE FOURTH PIECE OF BUSINESS was the plan that the Captain and the First Mate had discussed with the old Northern hands in the Puffin Islands, the plan in case of desperate circumstance.

So now they directed the crew to unpack the mysterious extra equipment and ironmongery they'd taken aboard according to advice.

As the sailors assembled the parts, Tom sat atop a cask of fresh water in the hold to watch without getting in the way. At first he didn't know what they were making (and neither did the sailors): there were wooden platforms and long metal runners, and leather harnesses.

Finally Tom cried, "Sledges! You've made sledges!" But

the crew looked around at each other, still not sure what they were for.

"Well, here it is," explained the First Mate. "Half the crew – and that'll include the sailors who still feel their wounds and you, young Tom – will stay here with the ship and most of the provisions. And the other half – and that'll include me – will divide up the rest of the stores and take them on these sledges in teams of two."

The sailors crowded round for further explanations, while the First Mate retied the knot in his pigtail and fitted an ice pick to the bottom of his spare wooden leg. But it was the Captain who said the rest.

"Each sledge will take a goblin-glim," the Captain said, "for they'll never go out, not so long as it's cold, and you'll travel the five Southern points of the compass until half your provisions are gone, or you run into desperate trouble, and then turn back.

"But I'd rather you return sooner than that, and bearing good news. For your mission is to find some Northern shore with better prospects for the winter. We want a place with trees or stones to make a fort for shelter, and wood to keep larger fires burning, and with luck, some game to hunt.

"Or if you can't find that, maybe a camp of Snow People, if there are any left so far north this late in winter, where they might welcome us. But most importantly, we want firm land beneath our legs.

"If you should find such a place, then race back to the *Volantix* with all dispatch, for it will be perilous for us to winter here on the ice, which might crack or split or crush our ship." The Captain stopped then, and looked at his crew, who looked variously sombre, scared, or determined, according to their characters.

"Cook," he said, "two helpings all round of something special tonight, and make it hot."

"WELL, IT'S *blobsterdis* TONIGHT," the Cook told the crew that evening, "in honour of our doom coming to fruition." (He restrained himself and said nothing about the likelihood of meeting ice trolls.)

Most of the others only shook their heads, long used to the Cook's dire pronouncements, and some chaffed him over it, while Tom only stared down at the piping-hot food quivering on his plate and wondered if the Cook were right. For Jenny too had said they would likely find their doom in the icy North, and certainly the *Volantix* itself was already held in the grip of the ice. What would she say now, when the Exploration, already stopped cold, had reduced its hope to the plan for desperate circumstance?

While the sailors about him argued about whether they were doomed, Tom remembered Jenny's story of Maxim Tortuca, a sailor whose ship sank beneath him and who swam alone in the open sea for three days until a giant sea turtle rose beneath his feet and bore him across the water to find his fortune. *"That was a proper Explorer,"* Jenny always said, *"who never lost hope, no matter how dismal and absurd."*

"Well, we're under a cloud at the very least," the Cook was saying.

"Under the Hall of the Stars, more like," the First Mate said, "Where sits the Queen on her velvet throne, who keeps her –" and he paused to make sure everyone caught the word "– her astronomical *stelliWcations* in order that they might guide sailors such as we."

But after all this, the sailors from the poop deck were not convinced. "Doomed!" they wailed. "Doomed! We're all going to die!"

"Well, of course," the Cook said calmly. "Told you that at the beginning. Now shut up and eat your blobsterdis."

"We're all going to die!" the two sailors moaned as they shook, while they stared at the shaking blobsterdis and tried to work out how it should be eaten.

Tom's eyes grew wide. "Are we doomed?" he asked the First Mate.

"My friend the Cook has a morbid soul, from the inevitability of culinary mishaps at sea," replied the First Mate. "If we were doomed, would I be leaving you my parrot for safekeeping?"

"Doomed!" repeated the parrot cheerfully. "Ding-dong!"

N

So the crew made the sledges ready, and the healthy sailors picked themselves off into pairs and drew

The Trial of the Ice

lots as to which way they would strike out.

At last, when all was set, the First Mate wrapped the parrot snugly in his shawl and gave him to Tom for looking after. Then he and the Cook, whose wooden legs were on opposite sides, so they made a good team, like partners in a three-legged race, put their shoulders to the harness of their sledge. "Just as I foretold," the Cook announced with some relish. "Skating on the ice until we freeze."

But the First Mate paid no attention and only said, "Well, we're ready."

Then all the sailors who were going on the sledges stood in their harnesses. They shifted from one foot to the other because they were cold, and because they were nervous – especially the two sailors from the poop deck, who were heading South-Southeast, which they had decided was an especially doomed direction – and waited for the last words from the Captain.

"Now I'm sorry I'm Captain," he said, "for you are the real Explorers now, while I must stay with the ship. But good luck and crack on with all speed, and remember your fellows left behind on the *Volantix*, for you may be the ones who save this Exploration."

Then the Captain and young Tom and all the other sailors who had to stay behind cried their mates off with three "Hurrays!" and three "Huzzahs!" And the First Mate and the Cook and the other Explorers began to make their way to points South, pulling their sledges behind them.

The Voyage North

The sailors left behind stood on the ice in the cold and watched the teams of Explorers spread out in a great half-circle as they pulled away from the ship, until the goblin-glims on their sledges disappeared in the Arctic darkness. And Tom wondered if he would ever see any of them again.

IT WAS A QUIET COMPANY aboard the *Volantix* that night, for they missed the others already, and none was more sombre than the Captain. For he had sent away half his crew into the unknown cold, and didn't know if they would return to the ship, or only find their doom.

There in the hold, Tom and the sailors who had remained to nurse their wounds were all quiet too, sitting amidst the barrels and casks of supplies, and wondering what would become of their friends out on the ice. And since there was no wind, there was no sound at all, just the sad Arctic stillness, and the small noises from the stove.

When the Captain finally looked up, he checked to make sure the First Mate's parrot was settled comfortably on Tom's shoulder, and said, "Let's have some music now; that's the cure for melancholy."

Then they all unpacked their instruments. For it's little known but true that on calm days time lies heavily on a sailor's hands, and most of them had learned to play a fiddle, a flute, or a horn, if only to while the time away.

So that night they sat round the stove and practised a long piece with many parts that the Captain taught them, but that Tom (who beat the drum) and the others had never heard before.

Just practising it kept the awful silence away. When they had learned the tune properly, they played it all the way through – "with all sheets flying," as the Captain said. And the whole ship rang with sound.

Sometimes the tune rose in a way that made tears start in Tom's eyes, and sometimes it was grim and frightening, but then one of the fiddles would take up a strain that would defy all the sadness and terror and made him feel that the world and all its flaws was triumph enough, and left him content.

80

IT'S A FUNNY THING, but the music in the hold of the *Volantix* made the whole ship quiver, as though it were one giant violin. The music travelled across the flat ice for hundreds and hundreds of miles, until even the Snow People in their domed houses heard it and wondered, and sometimes talk of it still. And the music rose up too, perhaps to the Hall of the Stars, for the fire seemed to dance in the sky that night like an echo of the symphony.

But even if it was only music, the Captain's tune did this much: while the sailors played it, the eerie quiet was lifted, and they forgot about the pain of their wounds, and they forgot they were marooned in the ice, and they forgot to worry about their friends who were gone in the sledges.

And miles away on the dark ice, the Explorers who had

taken the sledges heard the symphony too, and took comfort, although the Cook and the First Mate between them had some caustic things to say about the Captain's fingerwork as they stumped along.

BACK IN THE HOLD OF THE *Volantix,* when the music was done, Tom and the Captain and the other sailors laid down their instruments. Then they just stared quietly into the fire burning in the galley stove, until they all fell asleep without even setting a watch for snow-goblins, or ice trolls, or whatever else might be creeping on the dark frozen sea.

And all through the night they dreamt of spice winds and warm waters and lazy islands that bloom like summer flowers, and slept deeply until morning, when they were woken by a great hullabaloo.

The Trial of the Ice

CHAPTER EIGHT:
THE STORY THE TWO SAILORS TOLD

"*Hullo! Hullo!*" THE TWO SAILORS WHO HAD gone South-Southeast shouted from the ice outside. "Hullo! Hullo! Is anyone still aboard? We're back, is anyone left aboard? *Hullooo!*"

After all that shouting, the ship remained quiet, and the two sailors who had gone South-Southeast began to get a little nervous. For a wind had blown in the night, and gritty snow had drifted up against the ship and the goblin-glims around it, so that the *Volantix* looked untended and deserted.

"They're gone!" one said.

"They've left us!" the other cried.

"We were right! We *did* hear ice trolls muttering, and they came and ate the rest of the crew!" the first one cried.

"Unless it was the snow-goblins who came back," the second one said.

"Or the cold winds with the ghost voices!"

"*Oh no!*" cried the second one. "Oh no! I hope they were eaten by trolls and not taken away by the cold winds with the ghost voices!"

"What a terrible voyage!" the first one cried. "All that

we've gone through, and then we lost our sledge, and now the whole crew has disappeared! Oh no! What a terrible voyage!"

But of course the crew was fine; they had just been sleeping below decks, and now the Captain climbed out of the hatch and stared down from the guardrail at the two sailors. "Have you lost your sledge and come back already?" he demanded.

"Ah!" the two sailors who'd gone South-Southeast cried in fright, "The Captain's ghost!"

"I am not a ghost!" roared the Captain, so loud that icicles began to fall with a smash and tinkle all over the ship.

"Ah!" the two sailors cried in fright. "It's the Captain!"

"He'll roast us!" moaned the first one.

"He'll send us to the brig!" wailed the second one.

"No, I won't," the Captain said. "I tried to send you to find some better place, for there's nowhere I could send you that's worse than here on the *Volantix*, stuck in the ice in the Eaves of the World.

"So there's nothing I can say more frightening than this: come aboard and tell us what's happened to you."

THE TWO SAILORS who'd gone South-Southeast had a slow time telling their story, for they knew already they ought to be embarrassed, and they interrupted each other and embellished their tale to make it sound worse:

"Well, we started South," the first one began.

The Trial of the Ice

"South-Southeast," the second one said, to be precise, and to please the Captain.

"A good beginning," the Captain said, who was feeling more sarcastic than usual, "since that's where you were sent."

"Yes," the two sailors said, feeling properly rebuked.

"And then we hauled steadily," the first one continued, "except when we had to drag the sledge over a ridge in the ice, or bridge a crevasse –"

"Great crevasses of ice that open at your feet!" the second one exclaimed.

"And beneath them only the dark icy sea!" the first one cried. "And then, and then…"

"And then we heard the music," the second one said. "And we were scared at first, until we realized that it was only the sailors still on board, playing a tune." The two sailors looked at one another then, but neither of them said a word about the captain's fingering.

"It was after the music," the first one said.

"Yes, *after* the music," said the second one.

"It was after the music, when we started to hear the noise."

Tom and all the wounded sailors leaned forward at that. The Captain looked at them, then back at the two sailors who'd gone South-Southeast. "What sort of noise?" he asked.

The eyes of the two sailors grew round as cannon balls.

"A snuffling noise," said one.

84

"A shuffling noise," said the other.

"A muttering noise!" cried the first one miserably. "We thought it was *ice trolls!* Ice trolls muttering!"

"Ice trolls muttering!" added the second one.

"And getting closer all the time!" the first one said breathlessly. "And it was late, and we wanted to stop to make camp, but we were scared and needed to get away from the noise, so we dragged the sledge on and on over the ice until we came to another gap in the ice with the cold sea flowing beneath, and beyond it was a great ice cliff, and we thought, we thought...."

"We thought if we could get the sledge to the other side of the crevasse and over the cliff we might be safe," the second one said. "So we pushed and pulled and manoeuvred the sledge over the breach and the open water beneath —"

"It wasn't easy!" the first one said.

"No," said the Captain quietly, not so sarcastic now, "I know the task I gave you wasn't easy. Please go on."

"Well," the second one said, "we started up the cliff, with the sledge behind us, and that was even harder, and we often slipped and nearly fell back. Until we were almost at the top, and that's when we heard the growling."

"The *growling?*" said the Captain.

"We didn't know that ice trolls growled!" the first one cried.

"And it was right behind us!" the second one cried. "We were going to be trollibags and get eaten! Our doom

The Trial of the Ice

was upon us! Trollibags I tell you!"

"And so we lost our grip," the first one said, cutting in, "because we were so, well, surprised, and we started to slide backwards."

"The sledge was pulling us back," the second one said, "and we were sliding fast, towards the bottom of the cliff –"

"So we slipped out of the harnesses to save ourselves," the first one said, "and then the sledge, it slid all the way down the cliff with a crash, and then –"

"And then it tumbled into the water in the breach, and was lost," the second one finished.

The Captain was quiet for a while. "So the sledge, and all the supplies, and your goblin-glim were lost beneath the sea," he said. "And how did you find your way back?"

"We don't know," said the first one. "We just heard the muttering coming closer again and ran from it, as fast as we could. We ran for hours, until we saw the lights of the *Volantix*."

"Because we kept hearing the *growl*," the second one explained. "Sometimes it was nearer and sometimes it was farther, but it was always there, and we just ran."

"You were lucky you found the *Volantix!*" Tom said then.

"Yes," said the Captain. "If it was luck, or maybe the noise they were running from was coming here itself."

Tom put his hand to the bandage on his forehead. "Ice trolls?" he said in alarm, while the two sailors who had gone South-Southeast held each other and rattled like dice in a cup. "Trollibags!" they wept. "We're all for trollibags!"

"*Growling?*" the Captain said again. "I've never heard of ice trolls growling. But something's coming, maybe. So we'll stay near the *Volantix*, and that'll be the last night we go to sleep without setting watch.

"And you two," he said to the sailors who'd gone South-Southeast – and now they quivered like bowstrings – "Don't fear my wrath. For all the punishment you'll have is to take the first watch tonight, and while you're doing it, clear all this drift from the goblin-glims about the ship. But we've lost your sledge and all its stores beneath the cold sea, and we'll never know what lies South-Southeast, which might have been our salvation.

"We must hope the other explorers return with better news."

THAT NIGHT, when the two sailors who'd gone South-Southeast were spending their watch as ordered, clearing the drifted snow from the glims around the *Volantix*, they sent up a cry that woke the ship. It was only a moment before the Captain came out of his cabin and Tom and the others rolled from their hammocks and climbed out of the hold, but the two sailors weren't to be seen either on deck or by the lights on the ice.

Then Tom caught sight of them. "*Look!*" he called, pointing starboard. The two sailors were running North over the ice, already far beyond the last of the goblin-glims.

The Trial of the Ice

"Why do they run away from the ship?" asked the Captain. "What do they fear?"

Tom was sure that ice trolls must be near. Slush and snowballs for their insides, the First Mate had said, but terrible icicles for bones as well, Tom knew, and stupid and hungry and wicked besides. But he saw no tall ice troll loping about the ship, only something else, just as frightening.

For prowling just to starboard, beneath the leaning hull, was an enormous white bear.

"The bear," whispered Tom. "It was between them and the ship."

They'd seen bears, most of them, dancing bears at market days, not much bigger than a man and held safe on chains, but those bears were mere cubs compared to the white one. It could have been a great giant ghost of a bear, except that as it moved they heard tremendous shuffling and snuffling noises that sounded very alive, and the occasional curious growl.

But when the bear stood on its hind legs to look up at the deck of the *Volantix*, it was tall, vastly tall, fifteen feet at least. The sailors shrank back from the rail.

"Near three fathoms high," the Captain said in wonder, feeling for his sword.

The bear sank back down, and the rest of the crew started to regain their nerve. "We must chase after them!" they cried, though all of them still felt their wounds. But the Captain put his sword back in his sheath and stopped them, saying none of them would stand a chance against the great prowling beast.

"Listen, now," the Captain said, pulling off his tricorn hat and grabbing his hair in frustration. "Listen now, for this is an order: I've lost two sailors tonight, and there are four more sledges who may never return. I'll lose no more of my crew to this field of ice. No one is to venture off this ship except with my permission. Do you understand the order?"

"Aye-aye, sir," said Tom, and *"Aye-aye,"* said all of the crew after him, though plainly they wished to rescue their friends, as did the Captain too, of course. But instead the Captain ordered them to fire a cannon. That sent the bear lumbering away straight off, and they had some hope the two sailors would see its flash or hear its thunder and so find their way back to the *Volantix*.

And the Captain ordered that a cannon be fired high in the air every hour for the rest of the night, and twice a day after that, in case the two sailors or any of the other explorers who were away from the ship needed to find their way back.

All the crew kept a careful watch from then on, but they never saw the bear or heard its growling again.

IT WAS WEEKS before the other sledges began to come back, and each night they waited was longer and colder than the last. And the Captain always wished he'd spoken more kindly to the two sailors who'd gone South-Southeast.

The Trial of the Ice

Chapter Nine:
THE REPORTS
OF THE EXPLORERS

WHILE THE CREW ABOARD THE *Volantix* WAITED, marooned in the ice, the ship grew colder and her seams shrank.

Drafts and cracks the crew thought they'd already fixed opened up like old wounds on a sailor come down with scurvy. And when the wind blew, as it often did, it whistled through the whole ship, even the captain's cabin.

"It's a pity we couldn't have had the wind earlier, when we were trying to sail for the last open water," more than one sailor observed as they occupied themselves making the *Volantix* as snug as possible.

They held up candles and watched where they fluttered to find the cracks, then they pounded oakum in with wooden mallets, and sealed them tight with hot tar.

But no matter what they did, they were cold in the *Volantix*, unless they were right next to the galley stove, where (the Cook being gone) they were reduced to eating porridge and biscuits.

On deck, especially when the wind blew across the great field of ice and howled among the rigging, the cold was worse than they'd ever known. Then sailors would come back from a turn on watch almost frozen white, their toques and scarves stiff with frost, and shaking so hard with cold they couldn't speak before they'd sat by the stove a good half-hour.

Tom had it easier than the others, just because they made sure he had all the warmest clothes (only the parrot was warmer, for he had his own toque and shawl, in addition to being cosy and snug beneath Tom's jacket). And when it was Tom's turn to share a watch on deck, they gave him so many cloaks and coats he could hardly move.

Even so, if Tom's eyes watered, the cold would freeze his lashes together. And whenever any of them touched some of the ironmongery (as they had to, twice a day, to let off a cannon as a signal to any of the explorers), the cold metal burned like fire.

So they waited for the Explorers as they slowly recovered from their various cuts and wounds, and the Captain grew more grim every day, wondering how long the crew and the *Volantix* could suffer such conditions. Even worse was wondering how the Explorers were managing without even the shelter of the ship, but only the rough tents they carried with them.

But it was weeks before the other sledges began to come back.

THE FIRST EXPLORERS TO RETURN had gone Southwest, and they had to come back when they came to a great breach in the ice that stretched for miles. And by the time they found the *Volantix* again they were beat and worn down and thin from their exertions.

"All we saw was ice and snow, and twice a great white bear," they said, after a few hours recovering before the heat of the stove. Later they sat with the Captain and helped him fill out his charts, but now all they could say was, "Miles and miles of ice and snow, and twice a great white bear."

The second pair of Explorers to return had gone straight Southeast. And they had found nothing but ice and snow until they'd had to turn back because their sledge had lost a runner.

"And three times we saw a great white bear at the edge of the ice and sky," they said, once they'd warmed up, and eaten three hot dinners – porridge, biscuits, and salt meat – all in a row.

And the third pair of Explorers to find their way back to the *Volantix* had gone South-Southwest, until they come to an immense ridge in the ice that stretched for miles across their way. They knew they would never be able to pull the sledge over, so they left it behind and climbed the ridge, and when they got to the top they saw nothing but more miles of ice and snow, stretching on and on.

Going much farther without the supplies they'd left on the sledge would be impossible, so they turned back. And after days and days of tracing their way home to the ship through the blowing dark, huddling in a rough tent when the wind was high and pulling hard when the air grew calmer, a great crack suddenly opened in the ice beneath their feet, and swallowed them in the freezing water, sailors, sledge, provisions, and all.

Somehow the Explorers got out of their harnesses and free of the sinking sledge, and somehow they struggled up through the salty ice water and back onto the ice, but they knew they would perish of the cold in their wet clothes.

For they had no supplies or any way to make a fire, nor anything to light their way in the long Arctic night. Their alarm and despair were so great they were ready to simply lie down and perish when they saw the flash of the signal cannon from the *Volantix*.

The Explorers ran toward the noise that rolled across the ice in great echoing booms, until they collapsed under the lantern at the prow of the ship and were taken in by the other sailors and comforted until they were warm again.

"Ice," was all they said for a long time. "Ice and snow, and four times we had to run from a great white bear."

The Captain put them in his own bed with a pan of rocks heated in the stove to warm up, and then he pulled at his beard. "I sent out five sledges," he said, "and they have all come back with no news, or bad news, except for the Cook and First Mate, who haven't come back at all."

Then he sank his chin down, and Tom and the rest of the crew went silently about their work, or just sat and waited.

I must not give up hope, Tom thought to himself,

The Trial of the Ice

remembering Jenny's story. *For the First Mate and the Cook may return with good news yet. And if they don't, then there will still be the last chance: that Jenny may arrive in the Nonesuch to save us yet.*

But really, Tom thought their hopes were slimmer than Maxim Tortuca's had ever been. *I must not give up hope,* Tom repeated to himself.

The *Volantix* stayed in that grim mood for two days, until the Explorers who'd almost been lost beneath the sea were warm enough to get out of bed, and they heard the First Mate and the Cook cry, *"Hullo! Hullo!"* from out on the ice.

94

THE PARROT WAS HAPPIEST to see them back, of course, and for a long time they couldn't tell their story for all of the squawking he made for joy of being on the First Mate's shoulder again, and all the babbling he made in the strange island language he'd taught them all.

But the Cook and the First Mate had gone straight South, and they'd made better time than the others, for whenever there was a patch of ice they weren't sure of, one or the other of them would poke it with his wooden leg. If it plunged through into freezing water there was no harm done and they knew they had to make a detour. So they went a good way, slowed down only by storms and crevasses, which were problems. And they always kept their heads and stayed calm, being sailors of vast experience.

They went until they had eaten half their provisions, and even then they kept exploring, thinking it would be no great matter if they were hungry for a few days on the way back.

Just when they had gone as far as they dared, they came to the end of the ice and found land, though it wasn't the sort of land you'd notice at once. It was low and so frosty it almost looked like ice, but when they came close they saw it was really a shoreline covered in shingles of thin grey rock. So the two old sea hands pulled up their sledge, and took some of their provisions in rucksacks and stepped onto the island.

"It was a wasteland," the First Mate said. "Stone and blighted-like."

"And the wind prowling around us," the Cook said. "Carrying the sound of ice trolls crying our doom."

"Ice trolls!" Tom said. "Were you scared?"

"No," said the Cook. "No point if you're doomed anyway, I say. Though the noise did rather penetrate the bones. Begging your pardon, sir," he added to the Captain, who didn't like such talk.

"In fact," the First Mate said, with a look at his friend, "we saw no ice trolls, but the Cook only conjectured 'em."

"Well, what *did* you see on the island," the Captain demanded.

"There were no trees," the First Mate told the Captain.

"So it would be no good for shelter or firewood," the Cook said.

The Trial of the Ice

"And there was no game," the First Mate said.

"So there'd be no fresh food to be had," the Cook added. "Not so much as a lemming."

"Well, perhaps further on," the Captain said, looking up from the marks he'd been making on his charts. "Perhaps it was just the tail of a peninsula."

"Perhaps," the First Mate said as he drew a map, beginning with a large "X" and working outwards. "But remember, sir, we could only explore so far, for we were more than halfway through our provisions already, and needed to start back to the ship. For it's a fact that we wouldn't have had anything to eat this last week except that the Cook made us a sort of soup from our leather rucksacks."

"All cooks know it, and call it the Dinner of Lost Hope," the Cook said. "And we found something else which discouraged us," he said.

The First Mate nodded. "We found something grim," he said, and then stopped and looked around at the rest of the crew.

"Speak freely," the Captain said, "for we've all faced danger and terror together now, even young Tom, and can bear to hear the worst."

"Well," the First Mate said, pointing at the "X" on his map, "we might not be the first to try our luck sailing West through the Eaves of the World. For we found a mound of stones piled to make a barrow, and a large rock with scratching on it we couldn't understand, and we believe the stones were a grave in the cold for sailors long ago.

"And lying beside the barrow were two more sailors who must have been the ones that built it, for they lay curled up like they'd just passed away as they slept, and I don't know how long ago. For their clothes were odd, and they had these swords, and I've never seen their like before."

Then the Cook and the First Mate took out the swords they'd found and passed them around. They were well-made, but the hilts curved strangely like rams' horns, and marked along the blades was writing that none of them could read.

"These are fine blades, but I've never seen their like before," the Captain said.

"Nor I," said the First Mate, "not even in Wan-daling or Zunna-wundoor. So who knows how long those poor fellows have lain there, or what happened to their ship in the cold long ago, for I knew they were sailors by the knots in their boots."

"But they didn't find shelter by heading South, and I don't think we will either," the Cook said.

"Nor I, sir," the First Mate said.

Tom looked around at the grim faces of the Captain and the First Mate and the Cook and all the other sailors in the *Volantix*.

"Well, what will we do?" Tom asked. "What we will do now?"

"We will stay with the *Volantix*," the Captain said softly. "For she is a good ship and a lucky one, and has seen

The Trial of the Ice

us through many trials already. And I have strong hopes yet she'll see us through this winter and still be fit in the spring, or the summer, or the summer after that if need be, until there's open water for her to sail again.

"And then she'll take us through this passage beneath the Eaves of the World and drop down the other side of the West until she finds us warm waters and spice winds and lazy islands that bloom like summer flowers. And so around the great circle of the world until we come to dock in the harbour of our home.

"For I think even my first ship, the *Swallow,* will come home in the end."

But Tom and the crew could see there were tears in the Captain's eyes. And they fell silent, for they knew they were marooned in the ice in the most desperate place on Earth, and they knew that the two sailors who'd gone South-Southeast were lost in the cold and dark, and might never be seen again.

THEN TOM FELT HIS HOPE begin to fail, for try as he might, he could not believe they would be rescued by either a giant turtle, like Maxim Tortuca, or by Jenny in her *Nonesuch.*

And then Tom thought with a touch of fear, *No, the last hope is Kalifax, which they name me.*

"But one more thing," the First Mate said. "Five times we saw a great white bear."

The Trial of the Ice

"Take this glass and keep it safe, it shall be your present"

CHAPTER TEN:
THE TURNING
OF THE YEAR

IT WAS DARK NOW, DARK ALL THE TIME IN THE Long Night, though all round the ice shone faintly. The crew of the *Volantix* only knew day from night by the turning of the watch clock and the wheeling of the constellations. For each night the Great Way moved across the black sky like a long wave in the sea of stars, and the Great Bear circled the North Star as though it were watching over a cub.

Sailors on watch saw the Hunter appear low on the sky, and the moon rise and creep low along the south before it set – later each night as the weeks passed, and the year drew to a close, and their store of provisions grew smaller. Finally the moon disappeared for good and they were alone with the stars.

AND IN THOSE DAYS AND NIGHTS, the crew had little to do, save try to patch new cracks as they appeared. The First Mate carved away at making a scrimshaw from a bit of ivory to pass the time, but it was hard work with cold hands.

Now even when the air was still, the terrible cold crept

cat-like through the ship. For fear of it, the sailors gave up their hammocks – and even the Captain gave up his cabin – and slept huddled together with the nanny goat by the galley stove, so the cold would not take them in their sleep. Even so, only the ones nearest the fire were truly warm.

Young Tom fared best of all, of course, as the sailors let him tend the flames during the day ("For the Captain said you'd be our Kalifax," they said) and sleep nearest the stove at night, and he was still bundled in all the warmest clothes. But the cold seeped into the bones of the rest of the crew, and made them slow and weary and prone to silence.

And when they came back into the hold from a turn at watch on deck, the sailors no longer made any report, but just sat by the stove and shuddered, until they felt life in their limbs again.

Whole days would pass with hardly a word spoken, and when the sailors did speak, the words came out thick and slow.

Locked in the frozen sea, the *Volantix* lay silent, except for the creaks and groans from the timbers and the cracks and screams from the ice when it pulled the ship along with the motion of the living water far below.

N

SOMETIMES WHEN TOM was taking a turn on deck, keeping watch, he began to shiver, wrapped up as he was. His forehead would ache then, where he'd been wounded by the goblin's axe, and he remembered how the battle with the snow-goblins had ended, with him hiding and shaking in terror while the sailors fought on. And he remembered how the last goblin had been struck down and melted at his feet, and the cold fear he had felt at the icy water's touch, and wondered if it had been a sign of how the Exploration would end.

More than once when those thoughts came, Tom felt a wild panic begin to grow over him. *Run away from the ship,* Tom thought, *Wnd somewhere warmer and safer, Wnd help somehow.* Then he remembered the Captain's order: "I'll lose no more of my crew to this field of ice," the Captain had said. "No one is to venture off this ship except with my permission." And the Captain's stern words silenced the panicked voice, leaving Tom master of his own thoughts again, cold and still.

But other times as Tom was keeping watch, the fire in the black night sky danced overhead, and he heard its far-off crackle (though the First Mate said a more seaworthy term for the noise was *crepitation).* And then Tom remembered the story his Dad had told him, and wondered if the Queen of the Hall of the Stars ever looked down to see their ship.

Otherwise it was quiet, and the *Volantix* lay alone and forgotten in the Long Night.

ONCE THE COOK looked up, for he had intimate knowledge of the state of the provisions, and had been thinking of the future. Because he was so cold, he had to speak slowly and carefully. "Maybe the great white bear means hope," he said. "If a bear finds game to eat, perhaps we can too."

"Perhaps," the Captain said.

Then the First Mate slowly turned to his friend. "A surprising remark, considering its source," he said. The parrot turned his head too, but he had grown almost silent in the cold and held his tongue.

The Cook smiled. "It's easy to be gloomy when things are bad," he said. "But we can't all perish, or no one would learn about our terrible fate."

All the crew began to laugh then, some weakly pitching whatever came to hand in the Cook's general direction. And the Cook laughed too, until they were all exhausted by hilarity.

But Tom only thought to himself: *If the Cook has hope, there must be none left.* And then there was little else said, until the day Tom reported that the coal was running out.

"Should I let the fire burn lower?" Tom asked.

"No!" said all the sailors who weren't asleep. "No, keep the fire up!"

Tom looked at the Cook, who knew the measure of the coal as well as he did. "But we'll run out of fuel!" Tom said.

But the Cook was one of the sailors farthest from the stove just then, and consequently could do little more than shiver. "No," the First Mate said, "no, we need the heat, we need a fine flame, Tom."

The Trial of the Ice

Then the Captain stood up and roused himself. "We'll strip the *Volantix* of needless wood," he said, with slow deliberation. "Come on lads, stand up, be active, there's work to do!"

They took up their cold tools and went to work. First they pulled out all of the dunnage, the mats and boards that kept the cargo from rolling about in the hold, and piled it up. Then they knocked the tables apart and broke up the stools. They tore the doors off all the cupboards and took the staves from empty barrels. And finally the Captain ordered that they dismantle his private cabin, which was all, he said, just useless wood, since he slept with them now, by the stove.

The hard work warmed them up, and for the first time in weeks they shouted out songs, until there was a tall pile of firewood for Tom to feed the stove. "Let's call that enough," the Cook said to the First Mate, "or they'll want to burn our wooden legs next."

The First Mate laughed and called a halt, and the Cook served up a hot *scrummage* to restore the crew from their labours.

But all of them knew they still had hardly enough fuel to last the winter, and Tom was more worried still. For it seemed to him that if they couldn't find their way out of the ice when the summer came at last, and had to stay a second winter, they'd have to burn every part of the *Volantix*, until there was nothing left but the top deck and the hull.

The Trial of the Ice

Then there was little else to say or do, except feel the chill creep out from the frozen timbers until even their blood seemed to run thick and slow like cold molasses. For if any them got a scratch or a cut, it never seemed to open or bleed until it was their turn near the stove, where Tom still tended the fire and gazed into its flames.

In the flames, Tom saw pictures. He saw his home and his dog and his Dad. And he saw Jenny as she hoped to be, at the prow of the *Nonesuch* in a tricorn hat. What would she say to him now, he wondered.

"This is not," he could hear Jenny say, *"what I call exhibiting an absurd faith in good luck."*

But what chance is left? Tom thought. *If they call me Kalifax, what hope can I bring?*

Now the flames flickered high, and for a moment they rose like the peak of a mountain.

ONE DAY, after the Captain had fumbled through his log with cold fingers, and counted the days over and over in his head (which was a long job, for even his thoughts seemed to run slower) he looked up and said, "Tonight we must be as merry as we can, for we've come to the Turning of the Year." Then the Captain told Tom to pile the stove high and hot, and never mind the fuel, and he told the Cook to break out the last of the lemon pies.

So, cold and frowzy as they were, they celebrated the last night of the year aboard the *Volantix*. Tom made the fire large enough that they grew livelier, and they sang the shanty they'd sung as they pulled out of harbour, so many months ago.

They would have played their instruments too, except that their fingers were still too chilled and clumsy. And the Cook served out almost the last of the salt meat in a kind of spicy *farrago*, and two lemon pies, and a double helping of mulled port wine, and to cap it off somehow he made some figgy-dowdy and served it hot.

As the sailors talked, more easily and happily than they had in weeks, the Captain took Tom aside. "Tom," he said, "this is a year when Grandfather Frost may not know where to find you, and we lead a rough sort of life on the sea, and don't put presents in one another's stockings."

"I know," Tom said.

Then the Captain pulled out his star-glass and held it North so they could both see the Great Mountain that touched to the Roof of the World. He smiled. "We drifted while we were anchored to the iceberg, and drift even now as we lie locked in the ice," he said, "so I wonder how near we've come to the Great Mountain."

"I always wanted to see it," Tom said.

"That is too far north for mortal men or women," the Captain said. "But take this glass and keep it safe, for it shall be your present."

Tom held the ball of glass, staring into the little starry sky within, hardly believing the Captain's words. "But Grandfather Frost gave it to you," he said at last.

N

The Trial of the Ice

The Captain only shook his head and wished Tom luck for the Turning of the Year.

THAT EVENING, the First Mate finished carving his scrimshaw at last, and showed it around for admiration. "It's the *Volantix*, with the flames of Kalifax dancing in the sky!" exclaimed the Captain.

"I carved it for luck," said the First Mate, "and I'm glad it's done in time."

The Captain smiled. "Now tell us about the tiger again," he said.

So the First Mate told the story of finding his parrot once again, and this time all the sailors joined in when it was time to cry *Koway-roway-raro!* And then, full from their hot meal and their lemon pies, and warm from their two helpings of mulled port wine, they fell asleep easily by the stove.

But in the middle of the night, Tom woke up when the watch changed, and the First Mate and Cook came down through the hatch, white and shaking with cold. Tom saw that the parrot's green feathers had almost turned blue, and that already the sailors who were furthest from the fire were shivering again in their sleep.

Tom lay still then, but he was wide awake.

Not for the first time, he remembered how the Captain called him their Kalifax, after the magic torch that had saved the elves who'd tried to climb to the Roof of the World, and how all the crew had looked to him for good luck. But ever since the storm, all of their hopes, each more desperate than the last, had failed.

I have not been their Kalifax, Tom thought to himself at last, *And so we will never escape the frozen sea, but will perish here in the cold, lost in the icy dark beneath the Eaves of the World.*

Tom sat up and looked around the dark hold. He rose and piled the fire high (he threw on two table legs, a picture frame, and half of an old wooden locker), till it burned like a furnace. The galley grew as warm as it could be, and Tom thought hard while he waited to be sure the Cook and the First Mate were asleep again.

When he heard them begin to snore, Tom bundled himself up well in all his warmest clothes and stuffed his pockets with all the provisions he could find – ends of salt beef, ship's biscuits, and hot stones from the stove.

He gathered up some kindling and the leg of a small chair in case he needed to make a fire, and checked to make sure he had his tinderbox from Jenny and his star-glass from the Captain safe. Finally, he crept to where the Captain lay asleep and stole his pistol and one of the swords the First Mate had taken from the ancient sailors, just in case.

Then Tom climbed up and through the hatch, almost as quiet as a goblin, and found the sailors who were sitting beside each other by the mainmast, shivering and keeping watch, and he told them a lie.

N

The Trial of the Ice

"The Captain said to go below, and I'll keep watch," Tom said.

He waited by the starboard rail while the tired sailors went below, and waited some more, alone on the ice-shrouded deck, to give them time to fall asleep in the warm hold, so they wouldn't notice any strange noises.

And all the while Tom looked North, past the farthest of the goblin-glims that had been set around the ship, and hoped to see the shape of the Great Mountain against the stars. But the sky was thick and grey that night, and there were no stars at all, only a kind of inky black.

THEN TOM TOOK A HOOK and rope and let himself down the side of the *Volantix*. He crossed the ice to where the farthest of the goblin-glims lay, and picked it up to use for a light.

So Tom began the bravest and most foolish thing he had ever done. Tom started North, across the ice, against his Captain's orders, and under a sky that was absolutely black, on the night of the Turning of the Year.

CHAPTER ELEVEN:
NORTH TO THE ROOF OF THE WORLD

Tom walked North, away from the *Volantix*, towards his doom.

It was dark and cold under the rafters of the sky, and that night great shapes grown from the ice loomed strange over him, but Tom kept North, where no one else had looked for help.

Tom kept North, following the elves in the story he'd told so long ago, the story he told before the Exploration began. He hoped to find the mountain that touched to the Roof of the World, and climb high enough that the Queen of the Hall of the Stars would hear his cries and somehow help his friends.

For hadn't the crew called him their Kalifax, and always looked to him for luck?

Now and then Tom turned to look back at the circle of lights around the ship. There his friends still slept, warm by the stove in the hold of the *Volantix*. Out on the ice, the wind was still, and Tom himself was so bundled up that he grew hot as he hiked along. He pulled down his scarf and for a moment the wash of cold air felt good against his face. Only for a moment, before the cold began to bite at his nose.

It was when he'd left the ship so far behind that its lights were no more than a little glow in the wide dark, that Tom came to the great cairn the sailors had made to warn away the snow-goblins.

He stopped then, holding the blue light high to see the rough mound. It was made of all the helmets from the goblins slain in the great battle for the *Volantix*, and the cairn bristled with their black, twisted horns.

As Tom stood alone on the ice looking at the awful remains of the battle, the confusion of weird shadowy lines began to look like a great knot of handwriting. If the snow-goblins wrote the story of the *Volantix*, Tom wondered, would it look like this?

For the cold fear of the water's touch from the last melting goblin had never left Tom's heart. Even though Tom himself had struck down the biggest goblin of all, he only remembered how frightened he'd been, and how he had hidden as his friends fought for their lives. And despite the cold, he burned in shame to think of it.

If only he could climb the mountain that reached to the Roof of the World, and so make amends!

UNTIL THE CAIRN, Tom's journey had been simple enough. The ice had been rough and tumbled in spots, but Tom was always able to find a clear path, and besides, he was still warm from sitting by the stove.

N

The Trial of the Ice

But as Tom left the cairn behind, the last glow from the *Volantix* disappeared. Beyond the circle of blue light cast by the goblin-glim was an endless waste of shadowed ice.

Tom was alone in the frozen dark. Tom hoped he was alone in the frozen dark.

Now he was farther North than any other of the crew had been, and Tom grew nervous; for all he knew, the snow-goblins were creeping about the dark ice, watching as he left his friends farther and farther behind.

(But as you've heard, the snow-goblins were still hiding in their icy caves, gnashing their teeth with bitterness, and they would stay there for long years before they dared to come out and think of troubling mortal men and women again.)

Or what if there were ice trolls prowling about him in great long steps? Tall ice trolls with frozen tusks and icicle bones?

Jagged edges rose up that Tom had to climb, and there were long stretches where the ice had twisted and broken against itself in sharp heaps. Then Tom held up his goblin-glim and carefully picked his way among the rough frozen hummocks.

And as Tom went slower over the broken ice, he felt the cold catch up with him at last.

N

AFTER A WHILE, Tom began to lose his way and looked up to find his path by the stars. But the clouds were thick

The Trial of the Ice

that night, and there was no moon, no stars, and no fire that danced in the black night sky. Only a dark vastness that seemed to spin around him, faster and wilder the longer he gazed into it.

Tom felt like a bottle tossing in a wide unknown sea. He was dizzy; he almost fell. Then he stopped and pulled out the Captain's star-glass.

In the darkness of the little globe, he could see the pale gloom of the Great Mountain at the Peak of the North, though there were no stars shining in the glass sky. Tom didn't know how far it was yet, but he remembered the Captain's words: that even as the *Volantix* lay locked in the frozen sea, it had drifted farther North.

So Tom held onto the star-glass until he got his balance and was sure of his bearing, and then he made for the Great Mountain again, over the roughening ice.

And every time he stopped to check his course, the cold crept that much deeper into Tom's bones.

Tom crossed great stretches of the terrible, tumbled ice, all against orders, but always keeping North. And if he never stopped worrying about whether he was doing right, at least that kept him from thinking about how dangerous his plan was – and he had learned in the battle with the snow-goblins that dangers are more terrible when you have time to think.

As he went along it seemed at last that he was climbing more and more, that somehow the ice was rising as he went North, like the foothills before a mountain, and that

N

114

reminded him of the story of Kalifax and the two elves, and gave him hope.

Still, it was tiring, and after some wearing miles, Tom found a little hollow in the ice that seemed like a kind of shelter – if not from the cold, at least from whatever else might be moving in the darkness. He warmed his hands against the hot stones he carried and ate some of the provisions he'd put in his pocket: biscuits, and the very last of the salt beef.

AS HE RESTED IN THE FROZEN HOLLOW, Tom's thoughts crept back to the start of the Exploration, to the Captain's speech all those months ago, just as the warm summer was starting. Would any of the sailors have answered the Captain's call if he hadn't told the story of the fire that dances in the black night sky?

But he had told the story, and they had come, and now all the crew was likely to perish in the cold unless Tom found help. For they had always taken care of him, and given him the warmest clothes, and the place nearest the stove, and so only he was strong enough to try this last chance.

Even so, as Tom crawled out of the hollow and started North again, he realized how much warmth had been stolen from him as he rested. Tom walked and climbed a long time before he felt his blood run hot again, and still his fingers and toes, and the little part of his face that wasn't covered, burned with cold.

The Trial of the Ice

JUST BEING ALONE IN THE COLD DARK was frightening, but as the ice grew higher and harder all its heaps and valleys cast long, sinister shadows under the blue light of his goblin glim. And as Tom crept along, the shapes of the shadows shifted like living things.

My eyes are playing tricks, Tom thought, but every time he moved, something almost out of sight moved too.

The hairs on the back of Tom's neck began to rise. All at once he knew: somewhere among the shadows, someone, something, some strange beast, some snow-goblin, or – Tom's heart skipped a beat – some ice troll was creeping after him.

Tom had the ancient sword and the Captain's pistol, but they would be no match for the snow-goblins, if they came in any number, or the ice trolls if there were more than one, or the great white bear if it came by itself, and his heart began to pound. He kept moving, but quicker now, running and scrambling over the tumbled ice. And he pulled down his scarf and hood to hear whatever was following him over the frozen sea (though goblins at least never make any sound at all, no more than the falling snow).

So Tom ran North, panting in the cold air, until he crested a hill just as he heard a noise behind him. As he swung round to look, the shadows jumped and grew and Tom drew the Captain's pistol.

He waited, holding his breath. Suddenly a great creak rose from somewhere in the darkness below, piercing as splinters of bone. Tom could see nothing, but the echoes swirled among the tumbled ice, loping nearer and nearer, the endless dark closing in around him – until Tom could hear the cry of the ice trolls, until Tom could feel the cold breath of doom, until Tom knew the jagged tusks of the unseen monsters were reaching for his throat; until, blind, desperate, he fired.

The pistol cracked and jumped in Tom's hand. The flash lit up the ice far around.

But there was nothing to see.

And as the echoes of the pistol shot rolled across the ice, there was nothing to hear, except, just faintly, from miles and miles away, a whale rose to a hole in the ice and sounded once. That and the beating of Tom's heart.

Then Tom saw that he really was alone in the darkness and the silence. For a long time he stood, taking great gasps of cold air.

At last he turned and left the monsters behind, and started North again.

TOM HAD BEEN HALF-CLIMBING for a long time. He had no watch, and there were no stars in the cloudy night, so he could only guess how long he had been travelling in the darkness. But it was hours, he thought, and hours of pulling himself up through the rising jumbly maze in an agony of cold before he found himself come to a great crevasse.

Now Tom knew he had been going up, for when he

looked down into the gap, he could see no open water below, only a wall of ice stretching down as far as his light would reach.

The gap was farther across than Tom was tall – no easy jump on the ice when you're weighed down with coats and cloaks and all manner of equipment. Tom stood at the edge, considering his chances, for a long time. *I wish Jenny was here to inspirit me,* he thought.

And then Tom thought, *I have stolen this sword and pistol, which was wicked.* And he thought, *And I have disobeyed orders, which is the worst thing a sailor can do.*

Tom looked back south, where beyond the darkness the *Volantix* lay locked in the ice. *I have done these things for my friends who lie asleep in the cold ship,* Tom thought. *How can I turn back now because I am afraid to leap across in the darkness?*

So Tom jumped across, and kept on North. And came at last to an enormous cliff of ice that stretched up and away as far as the blue goblin light would show, its top lost in the darkness.

118

TOM RESTED AT THE FOOt OF THE CLIFF for a while, gathering his strength and courage, for he dared to believe he had found the Great Mountain at the Peak of the North, that touches to the Roof of the World.

He ate the last of his provisions, and then he fixed the goblin-glim to his belt to have both hands free. Tom reached into his pockets to warm his hands against the stones he'd brought, but they had grown cold at last. So Tom threw the stones away, and took his slim axe in his numb fingers regardless. Then he struck it into the ice, and began to pull himself up the face of the cliff.

At that moment, when Tom began his climb, the Arctic winds, which had been waiting quietly all this time, began to bite at last.

As Tom pulled himself by his mittens from one ledge to the next, the wind blew as if it wanted to shake him from the cliff. When there was no handhold to find, Tom swung his goblin axe into the ice again and kept climbing regardless.

But the winds shook him, and roared above his head, and shrieked with terrible voices over the edges of the cliff; and the cold no longer waited patiently to creep into his bones, but tore at him directly like a hungry cat who'd caught its prey. The words from long ago came back to Tom: *Winds so cold they burns you while they scream with ghost voices.*

And as the winds keened, Tom remembered the howling of his wounded shipmates in the battle with the snow-goblins. Then for a moment, as he struggled to keep his hold on the ice, he remembered the First Mate's story.

What would have happened to the First Mate if he hadn't outrun the tiger? And what would have happened to all the other sailors marooned with him?

The Trial of the Ice

IF THE CLIMB HAD BEEN EASIER, Tom would probably have lost all hope and given up. But he had to try so hard just to keep from falling down the face of the cliff, and was so beset by the howling wind and the blasting cold that he never had time to think.

So he went much farther than he had any right to, stretching and reaching and pulling himself up the mountain of ice without any thought of stopping or giving up, or finding a bit of shelter to sleep for a while, which would have been the end of him.

Even so, the little part of his face that wasn't covered got scorched by cold. And after what seemed like a long while of climbing, when the ice floor was already lost far below in the black night, his fingers and toes were numb with cold, and perhaps his mind was numb as well.

Tom was caught in a nightmare of cold now, creeping up an endless cliff of ice, with his goblin-glim like a tiny bubble of blue light rising in the dark sky; buffeted all the time by winds that tried to knock him down and cold that was freezing his blood. All the time thinking only of the next place to get a hold, the next swing of his thin goblin axe, which was only as far as he could see.

At last, by accident, Tom pulled himself onto a ledge that had some shelter from the wind, and some space to rest. He lay there on the ice panting for a long time, stranded high in the dark night, while the wind howled in fury for no longer being able to reach him. And after a while Tom had rested enough to be able to think again —

The Trial of the Ice

and that's when he knew he was in trouble.

For he'd stopped being able to feel his fingers or toes a long time ago, and now he could hardly move them. But he had climbed too far up to get back down. And still Tom knew he wasn't anywhere near high enough to reach the Roof of the World.

So he lay there, not knowing what to do, until he realized that whatever else, he had to make a fire, to warm up a little, or he would perish where he lay.

Tom pulled out the bundle of kindling and one small chair leg he'd carried all this way. Then he reached into his deepest pockets, where he kept his most precious things, and pulled out the Captain's star-glass, and set it carefully on his lap, and then he pulled out the tinderbox Jenny had given him for the Exploration. He did all this very patiently and carefully, for his hands were so numb and slow from the cold.

And then Tom began trying to work the tinderbox with his poor stiff fingers.

Tom struck once and he couldn't make a spark, and he struck twice and got a spark but couldn't make the tinder catch. Just as he was about to strike a third time the wind that had been blowing so cruelly since he began his climb finally parted some of the clouds that veiled the sky. And suddenly, up high under the stars, Tom could see the peak of the mountain of ice that he'd been climbing.

It didn't reach to the Roof of the World.

This wasn't the Mountain at all! It was only another

iceberg locked in the frozen sea, just as the *Volantix* was.

All Tom's hopes were come to nothing. They would all meet their ends here in the North after all. He would perish from the cold, here on the iceberg's ledge, and as the winter went on he imagined that the Captain would send out parties of sailors from the *Volantix* to search for him, and they would all perish from the cold in their turn. If the *Volantix* wasn't already so cold that they were doomed to die in their sleep, like the ancient sailors the First Mate and the Cook had found on the rocky island.

Tom stood then and held the Captain's glass up to look for the Great Mountain in the North a last time. But all at once, the flames of the fire that danced in the black night sky burst out, brighter and louder than they'd ever been.

Tom was so startled that he lost his footing and slipped, almost tumbling off the ledge. As he scrabbled at the ice face to catch himself, the Captain's glass and Jenny's tinderbox dropped from his grasp and fell over the edge. And Tom watched them float down and disappear into the howling darkness.

Tom already knew he was likely to die there, alone in the cold black night, far from the Captain and the other sailors. But somehow losing these presents, there at the end of all of his hopes, was too much to bear.

As he crouched there, shaking from the cold, he began to cry. He cried first for the Captain's glass and Jenny's tinderbox, and then for the two sailors who'd gone South-Southeast, and for the *Volantix*, and for the whole sad fate

The Trial of the Ice

of the Captain's doomed Exploration.

Tom wept as the light from the flames of Kalifax played over his small shape. And had he not been weeping so hard and so long, he would have noticed the sleigh bells sooner. Sleigh bells that rang out over the ice, coming closer.

Tom didn't know what they meant, but he got off his hands and knees and leaned against the cliff, his pulse quickening.

The sleigh bells rang faintly at first, then louder and nearer. They rang louder on the night of the Turning of the Year until Tom thought his heart would burst from joy.

N

123

The Trial of the Ice

Tom lay on the mountain of ice

CHAPTER TWELVE:
THE LAST ALARM
OF THE VOLANTIX

ABOARD THE *Volantix*, THE CAPTAIN AND THE crew slept long and deeply that night. No one was awake for all the food and the mulled port wine and the general merriment of the Turning of the Year, and the hot, hot fire Tom had made in the stove – no one at all, since Tom had sent the sailors on watch to bed before he stole away to try the crossing of the ice.

But as the hours drew on the fire burned down, and the same cruel winds that had torn at Tom howled across the open ice. The winds screamed with ghost voices and began to shake the *Volantix*.

With the cold and the shaking, the winds made new chinks in the hull, and they crept inside the ship, prowling among the sleeping crew like frosty hunters choosing their prey. Which sailor was the skinniest? Which sailor had the thinnest coat? Which sailor could they make sleep colder and deeper until he never woke again?

They might have caught the Captain, for though he wasn't the skinniest, nor had the thinnest coat, he was at the edge of the circle of sailors, sleeping farthest from the fire. But even deep in his sleep and growing colder, he knew the feel of his ship, and when he felt it shake in the wind, it raised a kind of alarm that called him up from the grieving depths of his dreams until he suddenly sat up and stared around the cold gloom of the hold.

"Who's on watch?" the Captain called out, and then the other sailors woke too. The First Mate looked around and counted on his fingers.

"No one, sir," he said, "unless it's young Tom."

Then the Captain pulled himself up and out the hatch, followed by the First Mate and the rest of the crew after. But of course there was no sign of Tom, just the bare deck and the open ice and the lanterns dancing in the wind.

"Young Tom told us you'd said to go below, and he'd keep lookout," one of the sailors who'd been on watch said.

The Captain's face darkened, and then he felt about inside his coat. "And he's stolen my pistol and sword," he said. "Oh, Tom, young Tom, what were you hoping?"

"The Northern-most goblin light is gone!" the Cook reported.

And then the Captain bowed his head in grief as he saw what Tom's plan and hope had been: Tom had gone North, to find the Great Mountain, in imitation of the two elves who carried Kalifax. The Captain's heart sank, for he knew the boy could never reach the Great Mountain, but only perish in the cold.

There wasn't a moment to lose: the Captain ordered two sailors to stay and fire the signal cannon every five minutes, and the rest to take up their goblin-glims. Then

The Trial of the Ice

he swung over the side and all the others after him and they began to run North, spreading out across the howling ice, crying *"Tom, Tom!* To the *Volantix,* Tom!"

The sailors made a good chase of it, a better chase than they had given the goblins, and even with the cold wind ripping and tearing at them like tiger claws they ran on till they were past the cairn of goblin helms, on till they no longer heard the signal cannon's roar, and only its faint flash in the dark, far to the South, marked the *Volantix.*

But they were none of them dressed half so well as Tom had been, and the Arctic wind drew the life from them like water from a keg. Then the Captain remembered with dread the words from long ago: *Winds so cold they burns you while they scream with ghost voices.*

Even as he ran with his crew, the Captain knew that he had lost Tom, just as he'd lost the two sailors who'd gone South-Southeast. And now he would lose the rest of the crew if they kept up the chase. So at last the Captain stopped, and called a retreat.

He yelled himself hoarse in the howling cold, as tears streamed down his face. He yelled though he felt his heart freezing with grief. He yelled until he saw all the blue and green lights of his crew, spread wide across the ice, begin to straggle back through the blowing dark towards the *Volantix.*

Some of the sailors hardly made it back to the ship, for at first the chase had made them warm, but then as they had to stop, exhausted, their sweat turned cold and

N

127

The Trial of the Ice

set them to shivering and shuddering. And others had great white wounds where the cold had bitten them, on their faces or at their hands and feet.

When they were all back in the hold (even the sailors working the cannon, who'd almost frozen from standing all exposed to the wind above deck), for a long time, none of them spoke, for the cold had drawn off even the power of speech.

"BUILD UP THE FIRE," the Captain said at last, "for it's burned too low."

"I will," said the First Mate, trying to get up. But then he sank down and said, "After a bit of rest." Then the cold quiet overtook them all.

Only once one of the sailors wept and cried, "Poor Tom!"

And after a while one of the sailors wept and cried, "Poor Tom lost in the cold!"

And after a long while a third sailor wept and cried, "Poor Tom lost in the cold, who was our Kalifax!"

But the longer they lay huddled in the hold, the less they made any noise at all, for now the cold was truly in their blood and in their bones, and they were silent and drifted in slow dreams towards never moving again.

As TOM LAY on the mountain of ice, with tears still

frozen on his face, and the sound of sleigh bells ringing in his heart, he heard a distant voice from far below, a mighty voice crying, "*Whoa!* And set and wait!"

And then he heard a kind of growling noise, and in the time it would take you to bound up the stairs, an old man was bending over him.

An old man, but huge of build, in a great cloak of white fur. He had tall boots of white fur too, and green eyes that twinkled from a red face that was almost hidden behind bushy eyebrows and the thick grey hair and long grey beard that showed beneath his hood. And he took Tom up and swept his cloak around him so that Tom was wrapped in warmth and the smell of woodsmoke and pine needles, and then the old man carried him lightly down the mountain of ice in six great steps.

At the bottom, where Tom had started his climb so long ago, Grandfather Frost lifted Tom up beside him at the head of a vast sleigh, tucked warm furs around him, and shook the reins. And as the sleigh began to move, Tom heard the bells begin to jingle again, and exhausted as he was, and falling asleep fast in the deep warmth of the fur, he smiled to hear them.

For a while Tom slept as the sleigh ran easily over the rough hills of ice, growing warmer and stronger all the time, until he opened his eyes and looked up at Grandfather Frost.

"Father, the crew of my ship – they might already be lost!" he said.

The Trial of the Ice

"Very cold, I know," said Grandfather Frost, "and that's where we're running. Straight South from here?"

"Yes," Tom said, "straight South."

Grandfather Frost shook the reins and shouted, "Straight South and faster now, our last race of this long night!" The sleigh was pulled by two great reindeer, rigged out in red, and carrying many sleigh bells on their long curved horns. Bells that rang with every leap, and every leap of the reindeer seemed to carry them yards and yards with never a bump.

Best of all, on top of each reindeer rode another figure dressed all in white fur to match Grandfather Frost, and when they turned back to Tom they waved and laughed, and Tom saw that they were the two sailors who'd gone South-Southeast and then been lost on the ice. So Tom closed his eyes and wept for happiness, and slept again.

BUT ABOARD THE *Volantix*, all was still, and the cold was quietly stealing the sailors away, until suddenly the First Mate sat up. Though his face was so chilled he could hardly speak, he tried to say something.

"Bells," he said slowly. And then more clearly, "I hear sleigh bells!" And the Captain wondered whether it was true, or just a last dream before the cold took him away. But if it was a dream, they all shared it, for they all heard sleigh bells then, bells ringing louder and nearer at the Turning of the Year.

The Trial of the Ice

WHEN THEY WERE ALMOST AT THE *Volantix*, Grandfather Frost pulled up at the reins and the sleigh came to rest in a great spray of ice. Tom could see that the lanterns still burned bow and stern, rocking in the wind, but the deck was deserted. And he held his breath, wondering how his shipmates were.

But Grandfather Frost leapt onto the rimy deck of the *Volantix* in one bound and called down the stovepipe, "Visitor aboard and coming down the hatch!"

Down below, where all the crew lay curled up together, motionless from the cold, they heard the great voice boom and began to wake again, and then Grandfather Frost came down the hatch, roaring an invitation to a fine Northern Feast for the Turning of the Year. Warmth and light shone from him like lantern light. Warmth and light that poured into their frozen limbs until they felt their blood run quick again and all their hopes come back to life.

They looked in wonder at his great white-clad form and waited for him to speak.

"Children," Grandfather Frost said softly, "you have been foolish to come visit me in winter." And he looked around sadly for a moment at the ship's company, lying huddled by the dying fire.

"But children!" he cried. "It's the Turning of the Year, and I have presents for all of you!"

AND THEN TOM and the two lost sailors appeared at the

hatch, all clad in white fur, and bearing great bundles in their arms: cloaks of white fur that smelled of woodsmoke and pine needles for every member of the crew, and one with sable trim for the Captain, and fur mittens with hot stones inside.

And the joy and astonishment aboard the *Volantix* was complete.

THE LONG WAY HOME

This Sea is probably never completely closed

They sped over the fields of ice

CHAPTER THIRTEEN:
THE PEAK OF THE NORTH

T HEY ALL CLIMBED INTO THE BACK OF THE SLEIGH then, for it was a great sleigh, an enormous sleigh, and the two sailors who'd been lost on the ice got atop the reindeer, and Tom sat beside Grandfather Frost, who cracked the reins. Then they pulled away, cutting over the ice faster than the *Volantix* had ever sailed the water.

There was a strong wind that blew against them, and the reindeer raced the sleigh forward all the faster, but none of them felt the cold. Perhaps it was because they were wrapped in new white furs, or perhaps it was Grandfather Frost, who was so warm and ruddy that he seemed to glow in the darkness like a burning coal.

TOM AND ALL THE SAILORS were silent with wonder as they sped over the fields of ice, under the vast violet and green flames that danced in the black night sky. But the Captain leaned forward and spoke to Grandfather Frost.

"Father," he said, "how many knots do we make and what's our course?"

Grandfather Frost roared with laughter, and the sound

rolled across the frozen sea. "You sound like a ship's Captain!" he cried. "But I can't say how many of your knots we make, for your time is not mine, and there's no reckoning speed without time."

"No," said the Captain, "I suppose not."

"But our course is to one of my lodges," Grandfather Frost said, and his green eyes were almost lost behind a great smile. "It is the most Northerly of my homes, my truest home, and I haven't entertained there for many a year, but tonight we set a great feast in your honour, a feast such as I haven't served since my children left the North to make smoke and stone cities."

It was hard, Tom had already found, to feel anything but happiness and laughter around Grandfather Frost, and so many things had turned out well. But suddenly he remembered how he had left the ship against orders, and lied to the sailors on watch, and stolen the Captain's pistol, and the ancient sword, just in case. He turned to speak to the Captain, to apologize for all he had done, but the Captain silenced him and clapped a hand on his shoulder.

"Tom," he said, "I don't know whether your deed was foolish or wise. But to see you return in such a manner, and us all here, all the crew safe and warm together, where we were in such a desperate way before...." The Captain stopped then and let the words go and just laughed for pleasure, and looked for the stars and tried to calculate their course. North, he knew, and West, but mostly North, and among the flames that danced across the sky

The Long Way Home

he saw the stars of the Hunter, and close by the Great Bear guarding the North Star like a prize cub.

And the Great Bear in the stars drew the Captain's mind to the great white bear who had followed so many of his crew, and scared away the two sailors who'd been lost on the ice. He turned it all over slowly, and the Captain smiled to know that the two sailors were with the ship's company again at last.

As the reindeer pulled the sleigh West and North the bells on their horns rang with every bound, and so the Captain and most of his crew fell asleep, warm and safe at last.

They woke as the sleigh pulled up with a tremendous spray of ice, and heard Tom crying, "The Mountain! The Mountain that touches to the Roof of the World!" The Captain left his slumber to look up and saw a greater mountain than he'd ever seen, a mountain that was to the icebergs they'd sailed among as a whale is to a minnow. It was the Mountain whose shape he knew so well from his star-glass.

They had come to the Peak of the North at last.

BEFORE THEM WAS the most northerly lodge of Grandfather Frost, set at the very crook of the ice and the sky. The lodge was low and long and seemed made of snow, and it glowed violet under the light of the Great Bear and the twisting flames in the sky. Its Northern windows looked out over the Mountain, and they shone yellow and warm in the Arctic night, and were hung about with holly and mistletoe.

The two sailors who had been lost on the ice led the crew inside, still waking from their slumber. And inside they found a great long table set for them, and there were other guests too, but Grandfather Frost was at the table already, and sat at its head, dressed now not in white fur but in a great cloak of green with a crown of ivy and holly berries set atop his grey head. And he placed Tom and the Captain on either side of him.

Then he clapped his hands, laughing, and out came men and women in pointed hats and robes that were bright with embroidery in red and green.

"Why, they match my parrot!" exclaimed the First Mate, while the bird ruffled his feathers with pride.

"These are some of the Herders of the Reindeer, who live on the other side of the North," whispered the two sailors who'd been lost on the ice, and seemed to know their way around.

"They are friends of Grandfather Frost, and aren't frightened by him," the first one whispered.

"Neither are we," the second one added, very quietly.

The Herders of the Reindeer bore huge platters of food and served the guests dish after dish. They served them hot leek soup and mountains of venison, and sauce from red berries, pudding and custard and shortbread and the raisin dumplings Grandfather Frost called New Year's cookies; they served all manner of food in great quantities, and laughed to see how hungrily the sailors ate – you would never have known they had already had their feast in honour of the Turning of the Year.

Indeed, it seemed to Tom and all the crew that they had eaten their small plain feast more than a long night ago, and everything about the *Volantix* was like a dream they could hardly remember.

"How do you make these?" the Cook asked with each dish he was served. And, "What'll go wrong when you try?"

ON THE OTHER SIDE of the Captain from Tom sat two of the Snow People, who were also honoured guests, and they took extra helpings of all the fish. After a while, the Captain leaned across Grandfather Frost's green cloak and whispered to Tom.

"Somehow in this lodge I can make out their speech," he said. "But it's a curious thing. I've been telling them about our Exploration, and they mustn't quite understand. Every time I think I've explained, they just laugh, as if they see no sense in it at all. And they want to know if the First Mate's parrot will make good eating when he grows larger."

But the First Mate, on the other side of the table, heard that and roared indignantly. *"My parrot!"* he cried. "My parrot! Why he's worth any ten of the rest of the crew. Saving yourself, sir," he added to the Captain.

Then Grandfather Frost looked down at Tom and the Captain and around at the whole table, and he began to laugh, and soon the whole company, ship's crew and Snow People, and even the Herders of the Reindeer who were still serving them (hot grog and coffee now), were laughing too.

For the whole Exploration suddenly did seem like an absurd plan, but a happy one, and the laughter rolled through the lodge and up the chimney and over the ice until its echoes rolled through the hall of the Queen of the Stars, and the flames of Kalifax danced brighter than ever.

"Father," said the Captain, when he could stop laughing at last, and wiped the tears from his eye, "Father, how did you come to find us?"

"Ah!" roared Grandfather Frost. "That was a lucky story!"

CHAPTER FOURTEEN:
THE GREAT WHITE BEAR

"IT'S LONG SINCE I'VE COME OPENLY AMONG your people," Grandfather Frost told the Captain.

"For you have great stone cities now, and smoke and banging, and none of it suits me, and all of it frightens my reindeer. So I creep through your towns and farms only at the Turning of the Year, so that I can fill the stockings of the children."

And then he turned and looked deeply at the Captain. "But perhaps you've forgotten what it's like to rise on the first day of the year and find a stocking that's as full of wonders as a new world."

"No, Father," the Captain said, "and I can still count all the gifts you left me, as I told young Tom."

"Well, that's fine then," Grandfather Frost said, smiling broadly. "That's fine. But I know your people less and less than I did before, and so I wasn't sure. And I wasn't sure either when I first heard tell of your ship sailing farther and farther North. For I count myself at home under any sky where the Great Bear shines at night, but here, in the high North, beneath the Eaves of the World, is my truest home, and I like to know what goes on.

"At first I thought you might be snow-goblins, trying some new trick, and when I heard your cannons roar, that sounded snow-goblinish to me, the sort of thing I don't like to hear so close to home. So I put on my bear cloak and began to sniff around, and I saw a cairn of goblin helmets, and guessed you might be mortals who'd won a battle with the monsters, which I heartily approved.

"But then I saw goblin-glims all around your ship for light, and thought again: perhaps it had been a battle between the snow-goblins and the ice trolls, for they can't abide one another, though they hate mortal men and women worse. And later, when you sent out small parties to find a safer haven, they carried goblin-glims too, so I kept my distance, not sure what to think –"

Then Tom couldn't help but interrupt. "The great white bear?" he said. "Then you were the great white bear?"

And that's what the Captain had wondered too, as the sleigh had raced North under the stars and the burning night sky.

Grandfather Frost laughed. "Indeed," he said, "you could say I *am* the great white bear, and many other things too, if I put my mind to it. For sometimes, you know, to creep into a house I must be small as a mouse, though that's odd uncomfortable. But would you like to see me put on my bear cloak *now?*"

And as he spoke, Grandfather Frost rose to his full height and his voice grew loud and rough as he towered over them. Tom thought his grey beard grew longer and whiter too and his eyebrows bristled more than ever, but the two sailors who'd been lost on the ice cried, "Oh, please, sir, no." And Grandfather Frost roared with laughter, but kindly, and sat back down.

"So I didn't know what to make of you," he continued, "and time was growing short, for the Turning of the Year approached, and I had many labours before me to prepare. But I marked that you played music, and I heard a great symphony come from your ship that echoes still, and it sounded well, and I doubted that ice trolls or snow-goblins had become musical, for generally banging bones and clashing gongs at irregular intervals is sweet enough to their cold ears.

"But the one time I came close enough to see your ship, the *Volantix*, I believe –"

"Yes, Father," the Captain said.

"A good name, an elf name," Grandfather Frost said, and then he went on, "when I came close enough to see your good ship for myself, I had the misfortune to frighten two of your sailors away." And here the two sailors who'd been lost on the ice hung their heads and turned red.

"I chased after them," Grandfather Frost said, "for you must remember, it's long since I've had much to do with your kind, and the Snow People who live most Northerly of all humankind are more used to the white bears, and the Herders of the Reindeer, who are my friends, know me in all my shapes."

He stopped and laughed for a moment. "I'm sorry for

N

143

it, though," he said, "and didn't know how much I was terrifying them, but they ran for a long time before I caught them – very fast they can run – and only then did I remember to take off my bear cloak. Though that hardly made them less scared at first."

"You're an uncommon big man," the Captain pointed out, on his sailors' behalf.

Grandfather Frost nodded. "Ah well, we straightened things out in the end," he said.

"But why didn't you come back to the ship straightaway and tell us?" the Captain asked the two sailors who'd been lost on the ice. But they only turned and hid their faces in embarrassment.

"They were abashed," said Grandfather Frost, "ashamed at having run from their posts, and mortified by having been so scared of me, and couldn't face their captain and their mates, and so I let them stay with me. And finally knowing who and what your ship was, and having prowled about to make sure the other goblin-glims that moved over the dark ice were only carried by other sailors from your ship as well, I let it all be.

"For I knew your ship was tight, and that you were safe from the snow-goblins, who are still hiding in their caves, and gnash their teeth with bitterness for the drubbing you gave them. And I made it a point to remember to look in on you before spring."

Grandfather Frost looked down for a moment. "It was a mistake," he said, "and you suffered for it, for I could have done much to help you. But as the Turning of the Year draws close I have many duties, and I put it in the back of my mind and prepared for the great trip I take this night through all the countries that lie beneath the Great Bear.

"It wasn't until I was almost done, and had come back to this lodge, that I heard young Tom's presents fall from his hands."

"You heard the star-glass and the tinderbox fall?" Tom asked, astonished.

Grandfather Frost turned towards him and nodded. "For I hear when any present falls or is lost," he explained. "Anywhere that lies beneath the Great Bear I hear it, and this was closest to my truest home, and on the Turning of the Year. So I called your two friends and drew my sleigh on one more trip tonight. And you know the rest."

"SO WE HAVE YOUNG TOM TO THANK," the Captain said.

"Yes," said Grandfather Frost. "For I had no idea it had grown half so grim aboard the *Volantix*."

Then Tom spoke to the Captain. "I'm sorry, sir, but I almost forgot," and he gave the Captain back his pistol and the ancient sword.

The Captain thanked him and carefully tucked the pistol away. Then he looked at the sword. "I'm glad you never had need of this," he said. Then he said to Grandfather Frost, "Father, it's the Turning of the Year,

The Long Way Home

and you have given us so much, and restored our company complete, and we are only poor and starving sailors. May I give you this sword the First Mate found?"

Grandfather Frost looked surprised. "Why, that's a handsome gift!" he cried, as happy as a boy. Then he pulled out the blade and read the strange words inscribed on it. "An old blade," he said, thoughtfully. "More ancient than you would believe. But it's older than I am by many an age. How long those poor explorers must have lain there in the cold, with no one to help them. At least I can see they get buried proper. But that's a handsome gift indeed," said Grandfather Frost. Then he stopped.

"Why, that reminds me!" he said to the Captain. "I have something *you* lost!" And his green eyes almost disappeared in a smile he couldn't hide, and he reached into a pocket deep inside his cloak and brought out a small wooden ship and set it before the Captain.

The Captain gaped in wonder. "Are all my joys complete?" he cried. "Look, Tom, look, it's the *Swallow,* and see how fine her lines are, just as I remembered!"

Grandfather Frost reached into his pocket again, saying, "And young Tom, you almost lost two presents tonight as well." And then he pulled out the Captain's star-glass, and Jenny's tinderbox that had saved them in the great storm.

Tom had thought them lost forever when he had dropped them in the frozen night. Now he gathered them close, speechless with delight, and then he stopped and offered the star-glass to the Captain. "I think you should have it back," he said. "The only thing I used it for was to disobey orders."

But the Captain shook his head. "I have been given all I could want tonight," he said. "Except," and he looked down at the *Swallow* in his hands, and then back up at Grandfather Frost. "Except, Father, I fear for the *Volantix*, locked in the ice where she might be squeezed or crushed with none to look after her or mark her passing. May we go back? Not all my crew, for they've suffered terribly, but me and any volunteers, enough to watch over her?"

At that the crew began to pound the tables and shout. "We'll all go!" cried the First Mate. "Every brined, pickled, salted, frozen, and otherwise preserved one of us, for she's our barky too, who took us so far."

"And we've missed her," shouted one of the sailors who'd been lost on the ice. "And we won't have you leave without us!" added the other.

THEN GRANDFATHER FROST raised his hand. "It's a noble ship, the *Volantix*, with a good elf name," he said.

"But you may trust no harm will come to her through the winter. Be my guests until spring, and then I'll take you back to her, in time to see the ice break up, and the water run free to the West, and you can slip down the other side and sail on till you're far below any country that lies beneath the Great Bear, and then you'll have to look after yourselves. But you'll do fine, coursing through warm waters and spice winds, and lazy islands that bloom like summer flowers."

So the sailors cried three cheers for Grandfather Frost, and three for the *Volantix*, and the *Swallow,* and Tom, and the reindeer that pulled the sleigh, and everything else they could think of, until they got up and pulled out their instruments.

It was as they were tuning up that Grandfather Frost called Tom and the Captain aside and led them by candlelight into his study.

THE WALLS OF GRANDFATHER FROST'S STUDY were covered floor to ceiling with pigeonholes, hundreds and hundreds of them until they were lost in the shadows, each filled with slips of paper.

After a moment, the Captain said, "Like an admiral's cabin, fitted to hold orders and reports from all the ships of the fleet."

Grandfather Frost laughed. "I hope the world holds no navies with so many ships as I have concerns," he said. Then he said to them both:

"I have brought you here because each of you looked into the star-glass I sent and believed in what you saw, and so came to my home by the peak of the North at last. And now that you are here, perhaps you would like to see something else."

Then he pulled a cloth from a tall stand. A great dark

globe stood there, that glowed with a thousand tiny lights deep inside. "It's like your star-glass, but bigger," Tom said to the Captain.

"How far it must be able to see!" the Captain said, peering into its depths.

"It is like the star-glass," said Grandfather Frost. "For this is the goose and all other glasses are only its eggs. What would you see?"

Tom looked at the Captain, who shook his head. "Young Tom, you must choose," he said.

"Well," Tom said, "well, my home, then. My home, and my dog and Jenny, and my father. Can you show me that?"

Grandfather Frost touched the globe. "Look close," he said.

And the stars in the globe whirled and faded as the colour of dawn grew over the glass, and then they saw flames flickering inside.

Tom peered into the glass and saw the flames came from a fireplace with several large, stuffed flounder set in the wall above it, and a dog curled up asleep on a rug before. "It's Jenny's fireplace!" Tom said. "And it's my dog!" Just then Tom's dog flickered his ears and opened his eyes and looked out of the glass, his tail beating the rug.

"He sees me!" Tom said. "Can he see me too?"

"Yes, if he's a good dog," said Grandfather Frost.

"But where's Jenny?"

Then the flames in the glass flickered and changed

N

149

until they were waves rippling in the early light, waves that bore Jenny's boat as she cast her net in the sea. Then Jenny stopped and leaned over the side, squinting as she peered Northwest.

"Can she see me?" Tom asked.

"No, though she is trying mighty hard."

"She lacks her prize expanding telescope, which she lost beneath the sea," Tom said.

"Hmm," Grandfather Frost said. "But still, she wouldn't see you."

"And my Dad?" Tom said. And the waves in the sea became the rumples of a quilt, until Tom saw his father asleep in bed. "My Dad!" Tom said. And his father turned over, and smiled in his dreams.

"Thank you," Tom said to Grandfather Frost and the globe turned to night and stars again. "Thank you."

"And you, Captain?" Grandfather Frost asked.

"I was thinking of Tom's story," the Captain said. "Of the Great Mountain that rises above your lodge, and the elves who tried to climb it, and of their magic torch, Kalifax."

"Yes?" Grandfather Frost said.

"And they were taken up by the Queen of the Hall of the Stars...."

Grandfather Frost smiled. "You have an Explorer's heart to dare that," he said, and touched the globe softly, three times. "Look close." And Tom and the Captain bent forward, their hearts beating faster.

The Long Way Home

The stars in the glass grew nearer and brighter, until they shone like gemstones set in the darkness. They spun in patterns, or shot in bright arcs across the globe. And among them was a velvet throne, and on it a tall cloaked figure who guided the stars, a woman whose face shone pale and bright as the moon. *"The Queen,"* the Captain whispered.

"She is kind, but frightening," Tom whispered.

"She is tall and beautiful and terrible to behold," the Captain said.

"Mortals may not look on her face, but you are permitted to see her in this glass," said Grandfather Frost.

Then the Queen turned her head towards them and in her black eyes they could see stars and worlds and pity and doom all together, until Tom fell on his knees and the Captain hid his face.

"Is my judgment come so soon?" the Captain asked.

"This is only a vision," Grandfather Frost said. "One which she has granted to you. Be happy, not afraid." Then she tilted her head so that they saw her tall crown, set with a thousand jewels, and around her flames danced: blue and white, and violet and green, all twisting together in the velvet darkness.

"Kalifax!" Tom said.

At that the Queen smiled, and cast a handful of diamonds at her feet. The flames rose higher until they could see no more.

After a moment or two, the Captain turned away from

the dark globe and thanked Grandfather Frost. "For I won't see the like again while I live, except in dreams," he said. "But I must be Captain again and play the cello with my crew."

And as the captain left, Tom said his thanks too, especially for seeing his home. But just as he was about to go, Grandfather Frost said, "Wait, Tom. For I have a private commission to entrust to you."

Tom listened carefully and accepted the parcel he was to deliver, which was wrapped in paper marked with the sign of the Great Mountain that touched to the Roof of the World. And there was no more business done for the rest of the night.

N

152

BACK IN THE GREAT HALL, with Tom and the Captain back among them, and Grandfather Frost sitting again in his green robe, the sailors began to play.

First they taught the Herders of the Reindeer and the Snow People how to do a jig, and then a hornpipe, and there was wonderful merriment through the long night of the Turning of the Year. And because they were with Grandfather Frost, time ran differently, and the crew of the *Volantix* played and ate more, and sang and danced longer than ever they could manage in a week of their normal time.

They made merry until they found themselves one and all asleep in bed beneath deep white down comforters that puffed like mainsails in a fair spring wind.

The Long Way Home

When he held it right, he could just see a little glow

CHAPTER FIFTEEN:
THE COMING
OF SPRING

S o Tom and all of the crew of the *Volantix* stayed with Grandfather Frost through the long winter, till all their wounds were healed and all their sorrows lifted.

Time moved differently in his lodge, so that sometimes it seemed they'd spent whole happy lives there, and sometimes as though it was only one long night.

Often between lunch and afternoon coffee (for there were six meals a day in the great snow lodge), and after he checked to make sure he had the parcel Grandfather Frost had entrusted to him still safe in his deepest pocket, Tom would just sit by the windows. Sometimes, when Grandfather Frost was gone from the lodge, Tom saw a white owl sitting still on the ice like a lump of snow, looking back at him.

Other times, Tom would look out on the Mountain that touched to the Roof of the World, and then look down at the star-glass in his hand. When he held it right, he could just see a little glow at the foot of the miniature mountain in the dark glass, and he knew that glow marked the lodge.

And for the rest of his life, when Tom took out his starglass he looked for that little glow, and when he saw it he knew that Grandfather Frost was entertaining company, there at the Peak of the North.

SEVERAL TIMES part of the ship's company travelled with some of the Herders of the Reindeer on their sleighs – big, but not nearly so large as Grandfather Frost's – on long rides through the winter night. And they found the *Volantix* and resupplied her with coal and salt meat and lemon pies, and even new tables and chairs to replace the ones they'd burnt for fuel.

The Captain came back happy from these Expeditions, for though the *Volantix* was still furred with frost, she sat safely in the cold, as though the ice that had squeezed her before only held her gently now. And the new furnishings the Herders of the Reindeer had made were fine, he said, better than the old ones, and would make other Captains green with envy for their unusual carving and inlay work.

Once, Grandfather Frost himself took Tom and the Captain and the Cook and the First Mate, and some others of the *Volantix*'s crew, out on his sleigh. And they rode until they found the little rocky island the Cook and the First Mate had discovered, the island where the ancient sailors had fallen.

As seven ravens stood on the rocks watching, the sailors

from the *Volantix* built a second barrow of rocks there next to the first one, and laid the ancient bodies carefully inside so they would be next to their mates, and covered them over. Then they all took off their caps and the Captain said some words for the Explorers who'd been lost so long ago. "We were luckier than your brave crew," he said, "but rest easily now, for we'll finish the voyage in your place."

Then the ravens croaked three times, took wing, and disappeared into the darkness. As for the sailors, they were all quiet until Grandfather Frost's great sleigh took them back to the lodge. But that night they drank a toast to those they'd buried.

AS HE HAD EXPLAINED, Grandfather Frost had other lodges and other duties, so often he was away, but once as he ate a late snack with the crew of the *Volantix* (some of the Herders of the Reindeer brought in hot chocolate and jam cookies), he seemed especially relaxed and benign, so Tom asked him a question.

"Grandfather," he said, "what happened to the elves?"

Grandfather Frost stared into the fire. "The elves," he repeated, "the Old Ones, I call them. I will tell you about the elves: they are in stories, but they are never with mortal men and women any longer, for they leave and return to stories before you can find them. For that's where they'd rather be."

Tom was quiet, not sure he understood. "The elves

were here before I awoke," Grandfather Frost said, "and eventually my age will pass and I will pass with it, but the elves will not pass, for they have already moved to story. For the world changes, but stories live on. See even now, ages after the elves have left, what young Tom achieved because he dreamed on the story of Turiel and Firiel and Kalifax, which his father told him."

Tom and the Captain looked at each other, still not sure they understood, but Grandfather Frost would say no more that night.

So TIME PASSED, in its strange way, until one day, just at lunch, the crew looked out the windows to see the top of the Great Mountain glow in a brief moment of daylight. Then darkness fell again, but the company went quiet. "That is the first sign of Spring," the Captain said, "and soon we must leave this place, and return to our own time and our own country."

When Tom heard that he checked again that he had the parcel Grandfather Frost had given him safe in his deepest pocket, so that he would be able to fulfill his Commission.

And it was safe, and Spring was coming to the Peak of the North, though they had many a merry feast yet in Grandfather Frost's lodge. But every day there was more light on the mountaintop, and longer, till it blazed like a diamond that reached into wide blue sky.

Not long after that Grandfather Frost came in early

The Long Way Home

one morning, bending under the lintel and shouting happily. "It's Spring in truth and at last!" he roared. "It's Spring! Every year I know it will happen, but every year it's a surprise and a pleasure! Spring!" Tom drew out his star-glass then, and looked down to see its plummy depths turn bright like daisies and periwinkle.

OF COURSE, there at the Peak of the North, it stayed as cold as ever it could be, but the Captain grew restless, thinking of spring winds blowing about the *Volantix*, and it wasn't long before they bade farewell to the Herders of the Reindeer, who'd been such good hosts. Grandfather Frost took all the crew into his sleigh for the last time, and raced them along the ice, bright now in the midday sun, towards the *Volantix*, all new-fitted and ready to sail.

N

159

As they climbed onto her familiar decks, made snug and tight again at last, so she seemed a cosy home, they caught scent of a warming wind blowing. The last of the icicles were dripping onto the deck as they melted, and around the ship little streams of water had begun to run under great overhangs of soft snow.

Grandfather Frost leapt aboard to say farewell. "You've been uncommon good company," he said, "but now I have much work to do before winter comes again, and so do you."

"Yes," said the Captain, "for we hope to make our way home by then."

The Long Way Home

Then Grandfather Frost called them all by name, Tom and the Captain and the Cook, and the First Mate, and the two sailors on the poop deck, and even the First Mate's parrot, and all the rest, and bade them farewell and good luck.

"You're aiming South, and that will take you beyond my country, under strange stars where the Great Bear is never seen," he said. "There are no snow-goblins there, though I've head dire tales of the Boogey Pirates. But I think you'll make around the other side and back up home."

"HOW CAN WE THANK YOU, Grandfather?" Tom asked.

"Why —" Grandfather Frost stopped, as though the idea hadn't occurred to him, and then he laughed loud and happily. "Why, all I ask is you leave a bite to eat and maybe something hot to drink by your stockings," he said. "For the Turning of the Year can be a tedious long night!"

"Father, thank you again," the Captain said, and then the First Mate led the crew in three "Huzzahs!" and three "Hoorays!" (Though some of them wept as they cheered, not thinking they would ever see Grandfather Frost or his like again.)

"Remember my Commission, Tom," Grandfather Frost said. Then he cried "Farewell!" one last time, and leapt from the deck of the *Volantix*, and stood with his hand on the prow looking ahead to the West, where they would sail. Just then a great warm wind came blowing up

The Long Way Home

from the Southeast, ruffling Grandfather Frost's spring-blue coat and tossing his long grey hair, and they felt a great wave move through the ice, which rippled and bent around the ship, but still held firm.

Then Grandfather Frost pulled back his hood, and he seemed like a younger man, and his hair no longer grey, but brown. And he took his staff and smote the ice before the prow of the *Volantix* three times until it cracked, and a great spreading lead of open water appeared at her head, stretching West as far as any of them could see. Then he leapt into his sleigh and was gone.

Aboard the *Volantix* they had no time to mourn his leaving, for the wind was blowing fair and there was open water ahead at last. The Captain and the First Mate shouted orders until they were hoarse, and the crew raced to their work happily, lowering the yards and unfurling the sheets till the sails were filled with wind. And Tom climbed back to his crow's nest, and looking about saw far-off patches where low green fields bore small blue flowers, while high up, a great falcon looped in the air on stiff, pointed wings.

GRANDFATHER FROST WAS GONE, but they were pulling West again at last, to the other side of the World.

"Boogey Pirates," the Cook said. "They'll get us for sure."

The Long Way Home

He saw his Dad standing there, and his dog, and Jenny

CHAPTER SIXTEEN:
THE OTHER SIDE
OF THE WEST

NOW THE *Volantix* HAD HARD SAILING TO DO, for they'd learned how short summer was at the Eaves of the World, and they had to thread their way through narrow channels, and alongside icebergs and glaciers and growlers, and find their way into bays and out again. The air grew warm and then cold and frosty again before they'd finished shouldering through the icy narrows of the sea.

But at last the day came when they found the other side of the West, and the great ocean opened wide before them. The *Volantix* changed course to drop South then, and sailed peacefully through mild currents, less cold every day, until they came at last to warm waters, and spice winds, and lazy islands that bloomed like summer flowers.

THE SAILORS TOOK THEIR EASE THEN, and stretched out on deck and bathed in the sun, as if they could never be too hot again. And one day the First Mate guided them to a small harbour in what he called Parrot Island and they all went ashore to meet his old friends, who greeted them wearing nothing but grass skirts, flowers, seashells, and blue tattoos.

The islanders clapped to see the First Mate and his parrot again, and danced around him, and pulled up his shirt to see his tattoo, and called him *Koway-roway-raro*, remembering the day he'd learned their lingo and escaped from the tiger.

The First Mate introduced his friends from the ship, and the islanders were mightily impressed to hear them all say, *"Oola-woola-woona-hei"* by way of hello, and covered them all in garlands of shells and flowers. Then Tom remembered his manners and asked, *"Woola-honey-boola-woola?"* And it turned out they all did want crackers.

AND WHEN THEY'D GONE SOUTH enough, the First Mate pulled out a little bag from a deep pocket and told them they were privileged to wear earrings now, like proper South Seas sailors. So they all lined up, even Tom and the Captain and the two sailors on the poop deck, who admitted to being a little nervous, and the First Mate and the Cook together poked their earrings in. It hurt for a while, but afterwards they all wore them proudly.

THAT WASN'T THE END of their adventures, for they stopped in Wan-daling, and Zunna-wundoor, and bought mysterious charms, and saw strange grey beasts as big as houses that trumpeted with their noses, and flying fish that sailed over the deck of the *Volantix*, though none of the sailors could quite get the knack of using them for badminton.

And they repulsed two attacks by the Boogey Pirates, and rescued castaways from six different desert islands, none of whom were at all appreciative, which made Tom wonder if they'd gotten lost on purpose, especially since after a few days aboard the *Volantix* they all took their first chance to jump ship and swim for the nearest lonely shore they could see.

And they were battered by terrible monsoon storms, and had a dozen other narrow escapes. But by now they took such things in stride, and hardly paid attention, for they were eager to be home. And Tom never worried about anything, except the private Commission from Grandfather Frost, which caused him to check that he had the parcel safe a dozen times a day, plus several times in his sleep.

When they'd sailed West enough that they were East again, as the First Mate put it, they began to turn North. Then they set their course for home, and the trade winds blew them towards the lands under the Great Bear and the waters they knew.

ONE NIGHT, they were all below deck waiting through a gentle summer rain, and Tom observed sleepily that they'd done everything they'd hoped in their Exploration.

"For we saw the Eaves of the World," he said, "and the fire that dances in the black night sky, and the Mountain at the Peak of the North that stretches up to touch the Roof of the World. And we found our way through the icy narrows, which no man or woman has done before."

"Yes," agreed the First Mate, knocking out a walrus tusk pipe that the Snow People had given him, "though an old sailor might not say 'fire that dances in the black night sky,' but rather," (and here he paused proudly, for it had taken him the whole voyage to think of it) *"auroral coruscation."*

He gave the others a chance to be impressed and then continued: "And we heard strange beasts squeaking, and survived the ghost winds, and fought back the snow-goblins. *And* circumnavigated the globe," he added, casually.

"And we dined with Grandfather Frost, as his guests," the Captain added, "though it's odd how that's hard to remember; as though it were a dream."

"But a dream we all had," said the Cook, "and now I know a better way to make raisin dumplings, if this rain don't drown us."

"Yes," said the Captain, as they felt the *Volantix* rock on through the evening rain, "I'm mightily satisfied with our Exploration." And so were they all. And if there's a kind of craving to see the North in the hearts of men and women, they had satisfied it well, and none of them felt the call of the cold dark spaces again, not for many years.

"Except the ice trolls," Tom pointed out, "though per-

The Long Way Home

haps it's just as well we didn't meet any of them –" Then he stopped, for he remembered the two sailors who'd been lost on the ice had told a story about ice trolls muttering, and he didn't want to offend them.

"Ice trolls!" the two sailors cried derisively. "What are they to a brave band like us?"

THEY TALKED LATE, remembering all the adventures of their Exploration, making them into stories they would tell for the rest of their lives at evenings by the fire. But the vision of the Queen of the Hall of the Stars Tom and the Captain kept to themselves, and never spoke of.

So they sailed on through the night, and in the morning the warm summer rain stopped and they saw the harbour of their home, with gulls turning overhead and the sunlight shining in a rainbow over the docks.

Those last minutes, while they worked their way into the harbour, and tossed out ropes and tied up fast to the dock, seemed as long as all the rest of the Exploration put together, and Tom didn't know if he was more excited to be back, or just to have finished the voyage so successfully.

But he saw his Dad standing there, and his dog, and his friend Jenny, just in from her nets, and brown as a nut from the summer's fishing – though not half so brown as Tom was from the South Seas. And he saw them tug at their earlobes, and the back of their hair, and touch their foreheads, as they noticed his earring, and the long,

N

167

The Long Way Home

sailorly pigtail he'd grown, and the scar from the battle with the snow-goblins.

Tom checked one last time to make sure he had the parcel from Grandfather Frost safe, and then he could hardly bear waiting until the ship was moored.

Finally Tom could scramble down the plank and meet them on the dock.

At first Tom couldn't do or say anything, for his dog was delirious with joy to see him again and licked his face and leapt and barked until he had to run off a ways to regain his composure. Then at last Tom took out the parcel from Grandfather Frost and gave it to Jenny.

Jenny looked at the paper marked and sealed with the sign of the Great Mountain, and then she opened it and her eyes grew wide with wonder.

"Now I'm mum and deprived of the power of speech!" she cried. "For it's after being my prize expanding telescope, which I'd thought lost forever beneath the sea!"

And then she *was* speechless, and just stared alternately at Tom and her telescope, and the new engraving around its barrel – a line of dolphins twisted together, and one great bear.

Then Tom looked up at his father, wondering where to begin his story.

But Tom's Dad only picked him up and hugged him close.

"I'm glad you're back," he said.

YVES NOBLET was born and raised in France and attended the Collège des Beaux-Arts in Bordeaux before emigrating to Canada in 1973. He received a Diploma in Visual Communications from the Alberta College of Art (Calgary) in 1977 and founded Noblet Design Group in 1996.

He recently created covers for the Coteau books *The Blue Field* and *Buffalo Jump: A Woman's Travels.*

DUNCAN THORNTON is an award-winning writer who has written drama for radio, stage, and film, as well as fiction and non-fiction. *Kalifax* is his first book publication.

Born at God's Lake Narrows in northern Manitoba, Thornton is currently a communications instructor at Red River College in Winnipeg. He may be reached by e-mail at: thornton@kalifax.com.

Acknowledgements

The author wishes to thank the Manitoba Arts Council and the Canada Council for the Arts for their support in the creation of this novel. Portions of an earlier draft appeared in *Zygote*.